GET IT ON

J. KENNER

Get It On

by

J. Kenner

About Get It On

Skillful hands. A talented tongue.
Meet Mr. May.

Fate's been messing with veteran Tyree Johnson. It took his buddies in combat and his wife in a fatal car accident. But he'll be damned if he'll let Fate take his beloved bar, The Fix on Sixth.

For years, he's avoided being Fate's whipping boy through sheer force of will, and now every bit of his focus is centered on saving his business. Until, that is, the first woman who ever touched his heart walks back into his life—along with a daughter he never knew.

After years of loneliness, Tyree's not prepared for the

way Eva's sensual curves and sharp wit still capture
his heart and rekindle his senses. All he knows is that
for the first time in forever, he's found a passion other
than his bar. But one final twist arrives when Fate pits
the bar he can't bear to lose against the woman who's
stolen his heart. ***He's a master at red-hot
ecstasy.***

Each book in the series is a STANDALONE novel
with NO cliffhanger and a guaranteed HEA!

Who's Your Man of the Month?

Down On Me
Hold On Tight
Need You Now
Start Me Up
Get It On
In Your Eyes
Turn Me On
Shake It Up
All Night Long
In Too Deep
Light My Fire
Walk The Line

and don't miss Bar Bites: A Man of the Month Cookbook!

Visit manofthemonthbooks.com to learn more!

Kenner,

Get It On Copyright © 2018 by Julie Kenner

Cover design by Covers by Rogenna

Cover image by Periwinkle Photography

ISBN: 978-1-940673-75-2

Published by Martini & Olive Books

v. 2018-3-9-P

Chapter One

TYREE JOHNSON SMACKED the monitor of his piece-of-shit computer and glowered at the electronic squiggles that danced across the screen. He stood up so that his large body loomed over the machine. Then he narrowed his eyes as he aimed a stern finger at the uncooperative candidate for the trash bin. "Last warning. You think I can't have a shiny new computer here within the hour? Just watch me."

He heard a snicker and looked up to face the two women who stood in the doorway of his small, cluttered office in the back of his bar, The Fix on Sixth.

"You laugh, but I was a Marine. I know how to handle slackers. There's still life in this hunk of junk. It's just being obstinate."

"Are you sure you're not just being cheap?" Jenna Montgomery asked, her green eyes sparkling with mischief. She wore her shoulder-length red hair in a ponytail, making the smattering of freckles over her fair skin seem even more prominent.

Seeing her, Tyree reminded himself that The Fix wasn't solely his anymore; he'd recently taken on three partners. And a good thing, too. Only a few months ago, his blood pressure had been spiking daily from the constant worry about losing his beloved bar due to a balloon note that he didn't have the cash to pay off.

Then Jenna Montgomery, Reece Walker, and Brent Sinclair had stepped forward and not only helped him pay off the note, but were now working side-by-side with Tyree to make sure that The Fix was solidly in the black come the end of the year. That was, in fact, the condition Tyree had set when he agreed to take on his three new partners; if The Fix wasn't turning a profit by the end of the year, they would put it up for sale and split the proceeds. Because no way was Tyree throwing good money after bad.

Hopefully, it wouldn't come to that. He loved this place with its thick limestone walls and long gleaming bar too damn much.

He'd bought the corner property on Austin's popular Sixth Street six years ago after digging himself out of a morass of depression and pain. The Fix wasn't just a job—it was his life. Hell, it was his resurrection. A place he'd worked toward. A business he loved. A dream that had revived him after tragedy had cut him off at the knees.

And not just his dream; it had been a dream he'd shared with his wife, God rest her soul. And it was damned ironic that even after years of scrimping and saving, he'd only been able to afford the place after Teiko's death—and the payout on her life insurance.

He'd traded one love for another, but not a day went by when he wouldn't eagerly burn The Fix to the ground if it would gain him even one more day with the woman whose death had left a hole in his heart.

But that was impossible, so he was doing the next best thing; he was working his ass off to improve The Fix, draw in more customers, and sell more food and drink. Anything and everything to keep the bar's doors open and him standing stalwart over the place that represented a dream she'd once shared.

And if that meant limping along with a crappy computer, then that's what he was going to do.

With a wide grin, he caught Jenna's eye and then glanced down at the monitor, where the spreadsheet he'd been going over earlier now filled the screen, all bright and innocent as if it had never been a bug up his ass.

"See there? All good."

"Uh-huh." Jenna exchanged an amused glance with Megan Clark as both women stepped all the way into the office.

The second woman tucked a long strand of dark hair behind one ear, then pushed a pair of black cat's eye glasses up her nose. Both gestures seemed like nervous habits, which seemed out of character for the woman he'd recently hired as the bar's Girl Friday, gofer, dogsbody, assistant, or whatever the hell you wanted to call it. But before he could find a casual way to ask her what was wrong, Megan shrugged, and said, "Austin allergies. I don't usually wear glasses, but my contacts are driving me crazy."

He nodded, realizing that she'd misunderstood his questioning glance. Before he could clarify, though, Jenna jumped in.

"Thanks for doing this now," she said, dropping into one of the guest chairs as Megan continued to stand, leaning against the rough limestone wall. "I know meeting before the bar opens is more convenient, but I had a doctor's appointment this morning."

"Everything okay?" He fought a worried frown as he settled down behind the desk, noting that her cheeks seemed a little hollow and thinking that she'd shed a few pounds. She looked healthy enough on the whole—hell, her skin was practically rosy—but Jenna was a little thing, and if she lost too much weight...

"What? Oh. Sure." A flush of color crept up her cheeks. "Just a little, you know, nauseous. I'm sure it'll pass."

"Hmmm." He studied her, his mind whirring. "Don't let Reece catch it."

Her cheeks burned even redder at the mention of Reece Walker's name. Reece and Jenna had recently become engaged. And now, as Tyree remembered the nausea that had laid Teiko flat when she'd been pregnant with their son, he couldn't help but wonder if there was more than wedding bells in Reece and Jenna's future. About seven pounds or eight pounds more, actually.

Jenna cleared her throat and dug a notebook out of her bag. "We have a long list of things we could go over, but since it's working hours, Megan and I thought we'd only hit the top ones today."

She gestured toward Megan, who nodded, then shook her head. "I'm sorry. We need to talk about the Man of the Month calendar and the cookbook, but I just have to say something first."

She shot Jenna an apologetic look as Jenna rolled her eyes. "Jenna told me that I don't need to worry, but I wanted to say again how much I appreciate you giving me a job. It's not as if you have much call for a makeup artist in a bar, and it's really helping me out. I've only had a few makeup jobs since I moved to Austin, and that's my own fault, since I pretty much came on a whim. And money's been tight."

"Megan, come on," Jenna said. "You know it's fine."

Megan kept her attention on Tyree. "I know you

were working on the books just now. And I know that The Fix is doing everything to up revenue. I don't want to be a drain. I don't feel right taking this job if it's going to be a problem for the bottom line."

Tyree nodded slowly as he settled in behind the desk. "Fair enough. You've been officially working here for how long? Four days?" At her nod, he continued. "And in that time you've worked as a hostess, helped behind the bar, worked with Jenna on this calendar issue I'm about to hear about, made a Costco run for paper products, did a stint of prep work in the kitchen, and spent over an hour on the phone with the HVAC technician. Hell, without you, we might have had to close up. No AC in Austin during the summer? That's too many sweaty bodies in my book."

"All true," Megan said. "It's just that—"

"And haven't you been doing Brooke's makeup before she goes in front of the camera?" he added, referring to one of the two stars of *The Business Plan*, the reality television show that was also doing a complete makeover on the bar's interior and whose cameras had become a constant presence at the bar.

"Well, yeah," she admitted, as Jenna crossed her arms, looking smug.

"I'd say you're pulling your weight just fine, Megan," Tyree said. "And I'm happy that when you needed the extra work, we had enough to toss it your way."

He meant what he said. He didn't know the details of why Megan left a thriving career as a makeup artist in LA to move to Austin, but he did know that she'd done it at the spur of the moment. And that there'd been a man somewhere in the picture. Presumably a man she was trying to avoid.

He hated the thought that Eli might be in a strange town someday without work or friends to help him. And the thought was doubly potent if he imagined that Eli was a daughter instead of a son. Old fashioned, maybe, but that's the way Tyree rolled. "We square?" he asked, his attention focused on her.

"Yeah," she said. Her expression was firm and businesslike, but he saw the smile behind her glasses. "We are."

"Then let's get to talking about this calendar. I swear, Jenna, I never expected there'd come a day when part of my job would be looking at beefcake shots of shirtless men."

She blinked at him, all innocence. "That wasn't part of your Marine training?"

"Watch it, girl," he said, but with laughter in his voice.

"Well, you're off the hook today, because we have a problem. I'd hoped to have a few proofs to show you —just shots of Reece to get an idea of lighting and poses before we schedule the full shoot for Mr. January to Mr. March. But our photographer got hired by some fashion magazine, dropped everything, and moved to Milan."

"I'm impressed."

Jenna scowled. "He was supposed to be good. Now he's gone. So Megan and I are interviewing replacements and poring over portfolios. Fortunately, all the guys are easy to get a hold of, so I don't think scheduling will be a problem. And of course Megan can do makeup, so we don't have to worry about that. So by the time we hire someone, we can probably knock out Mr. April and Mr. May at the same shoot."

"We want to get the final, cleaned-up images to the calendar designer as early as possible so that we can stick to a late October on-sale date for the calendar," Megan added. "And we want all the shots to have continuity. Like writers, photographers have a voice. We don't want someone who's going to abandon us midway through the project. We'll be running contests into early October, right?"

Megan directed the question at Jenna, who nodded. "It's the best way to keep interest up and folks walking through the doors. At any rate, the point is we're looking for someone who can photograph both men and food. If we can use the same photographer for the cookbook, that would be sweet. You're working on the recipes, right?"

She tilted her head as she eyed him, and he was reminded of Mrs. Thibodeaux, his fourth grade teacher in New Orleans.

"Got a stack of them in this pile of junk," he said, tapping his computer affectionately.

Jenna nodded, the gesture obviously a mental checkmark, and continued. "So that's the scoop on the end result. Meanwhile, Megan and I both think we need to kick up the real estate on the actual contest."

Tyree's brows rose. "Real estate?"

"Male pecs, male abs, male torso. You know. The reason the women come every other Wednesday."

"We want to lure in some new guys," Jenna explained, probably in response to his confused expression. "High profile guys. Nolan's a great start," she said, referring to a local drive-time radio personality who would be bounding across the stage in two days for the Mr. April contest, "but we want to go even further."

"You have ideas as to where to find these amazing paragons of manhood?"

Jenna's lips twitched. "I think you should enter. Megan agrees," she added, as her companion nodded.

Tyree crossed his arms over his massive chest, leaned back in his chair, and shook his head. "I'll be forty-six in a few months. I may not be too old to sponsor that shit, but I'm definitely too old to participate."

The women exchanged looks. "The female point of view begs to differ, but we can table it for right now. The point is, we're going to go hot and heavy into recruiting. Megan has a few ideas on which local businessmen to approach. The kind who look very fine in tailored suits. And we're thinking a wet T-shirt contest might be fun."

Tyree leaned back and lifted his eyes to heaven. "Lord, save me from ambitious women."

"Funny," Jenna said, as Tyree grinned.

"Seriously, Jen, this is your concept, your baby. You run it how you want, and I'll support you. Anything else?"

"Just that we'll keep bugging you about entering. You've got some serious pecs, bossman. And the broadest shoulders I've ever seen. You're almost as hot as Reece," she teased as she pushed herself up out of her chair.

He just shook his head and chuckled.

"Eventually we'll wear you down," Megan promised. Or maybe it was a threat.

"And one day hell will freeze over," Tyree shot back. "Doesn't mean either of us will be around to see it."

She laughed, and the two women hustled out leaving Tyree shaking his head, amused.

Since he'd managed to scare his computer into cooperating, Tyree worked a bit more on the accounts, and found that his mood had improved. Probably a little bit because of Jenna and Megan's company, but also because the books were showing a consistent increase in revenue over the past few weeks. And that was a hell of a thing.

He shut the machine down before it had the chance to get cranky again, then headed into the kitchen to make sure things were running smoothly, and the team wasn't getting backed up with the lunchtime rush.

During the first four years that The Fix had been open, Tyree himself had run the kitchen, experimenting as he finalized what he now considered to be a damn perfect menu. But with the increasing competition on Sixth Street, the heart of Austin's tourist-and-college scene, he'd made the decision to be a front-of-the-bar owner, getting to know the customers and having a presence in the place. That was something a corporate bar could never replicate. That true down-home feel of a genuine local bar.

Since Jenna had come on board as the bar's marketing guru, she'd seconded his decision. And although Tyree missed being in the kitchen trying to replicate and expand on the southern flavors of his childhood, he couldn't deny that he liked the sense of being at the center of life at The Fix.

"Easton," Tyree said, clapping the local lawyer on the back as he nodded toward the beer. "I'm guessing no court this afternoon."

"You guessed right. I'm about to head back to my office, let my paralegal load me down with folders, then grab a taxi to the airport. Three days of depositions in Lansing. It's going to be brutal."

"At least you won't have to come up with an excuse for Megan as to why you're not entered in the Mr. April or Mr. May contest."

Easton's eyes widened. "She's on a rampage?"

"Be wary, my friend," Tyree said, chuckling as he moved down the bar to greet some other customers, then say a few words to Eric, the bartender working the lunch shift. He was leaning forward to ask Eric if he could pick up an extra shift when something—or rather, someone—snagged his attention.

It was just a feeling. Just the oddest sense of familiarity. Hell, he hadn't even been looking toward the door, so the girl was only at the edge of his periphery.

It didn't matter. She compelled him. And he stopped what he was doing, then turned toward the entrance.

Eva?

But no, that was absurd, and the ridiculous moment passed as quickly as it had come. Of course it wasn't Eva. How could it be? She was halfway across the country and more than two decades away. Even if she'd walked through that door, they were separated by time and space. By pain and death. By life and dreams and family and loss.

The current of life moved on, and his current had pushed him past Eva a long, long time ago. And that was a good thing, too. Otherwise he never would have met Teiko, the wife he adored. The mother of his son.

And yet the girl by the door had captured his attention…

Not a doppelgänger—not identical at all. But damned if there wasn't a striking similarity. The same shade of dark skin, like coffee with just a few drops of cream. The mouth that flashed a wide, easy smile. The close-cropped hair with deliberately placed curls at her forehead and in front of her ears. A sleek, sophisticated style that accentuated those wide eyes and high cheekbones.

Pushed forward by both curiosity and trepidation, Tyree took a step toward her, only to find his path blocked by Tiffany Russell, one of his best waitresses, who was looking both frazzled and uncertain.

"Tiffany? What's the matter?"

"I need—" Her voice dropped to a whisper. "Oh, hell. Can I talk to you? Maybe over in the back bar?"

The Fix on Sixth boasted two bar areas. A front area with more seating and a stage that played host to local bands. And a smaller back bar, with just a few tables and a much more intimate feel. Since she was clearly agitated, he followed her to the back, his concern mounting.

"What's going on?" he asked, as soon as they were standing near the windows in the back bar. They were out of earshot of the customers, most of whom were sitting on stools at the polished bar, chatting with Lori, one of The Fix's first shift bartenders.

"I just thought you should know that Steven Kane—you know him, right? The manager at Bodacious?" At Tyree's nod, she continued. "Well, he cornered me at Starbucks the other day and started chatting me up about how it was to work here, and if I got paid enough, and how much is the door on the nights we do the Man of the Month contest."

Tyree said nothing. He was too busy fuming. Not about the fact that Bodacious—one of the corporate bullshit bars that had moved in down the street with watered down dollar drinks—was asking about the competition and earnings. No, what pissed Tyree off was that they were trying to poach his employees.

"I didn't tell him anything," Tiffany said, looking a little taken aback by Tyree's silence. "And honestly I don't care what you pay me. I love working here, and I'm not dressing like a damn hooker just for better tips." He chuckled, and she frowned. "Just don't, you know, knock my wage down by a dollar."

"Wouldn't do that," Tyree said. "And I appreciate the loyalty." Which was true. Even though he suspected that she was more loyal to her not-so-secret crush on Eric than she was to him.

"You've got it in spades. But here's the thing." She bent in closer, as if the patrons at the bar might give a rat's ass about their conversation. "I think they're hitting on Aly, too. And I know she's hard up for cash. I think she might bail on us."

Shit.

Aly was a waitress who Tyree had recently trained and promoted to bartender. And goddamn Steven Kane if he poached her away from him.

"I don't know for sure," Tiffany said. "I just thought you should—"

Since she looked to be on the verge of tears—and Tyree really couldn't handle any tears today—he put his hand firmly on her shoulder. "It's okay. You just take care of those customers and let me worry about it, okay?"

She nodded, drew in a breath, and started for the main room.

"And Tiffany?"

She looked back over her shoulder.

"You did right letting me know."

He saw the relief wash over her face, and felt a bit relieved himself. That was one good deed he'd done today. If he killed Kane, would that erase all his good karma? He scowled, considering. Probably better to let the little prick keep breathing. But it was a damn close call.

As he headed back into the main bar area, he found himself casting his gaze around in search of the woman who looked so much like Eva. She wasn't there, and as he continued toward his office, he couldn't shake the lingering disappointment.

Back at his desk, he tried to concentrate on all the mundane tasks that needed attention, but he couldn't focus. Instead, all his attention was taken by the framed photo on his desk. A silly shot of a nine-year-old Elijah goofing around with Teiko in the backyard.

Tyree had been on the back patio fighting with the camera, and when he'd finally gotten the settings right, he'd called her name. She'd looked over at him, her arms around the squirming boy and her eyes filled with so much love he'd almost frozen instead of clicking the shutter.

It was one of the last photos he'd taken of her.

His chest tightened as the memory crashed hard over him. Christ, he loved her.

Gently, he brushed a fingertip over the image of her face. "I miss you, babe," he murmured, then pushed away from the desk and stood.

According to the clock in the shape of a beer bottle that was mounted on the office wall, it was earlier than he'd planned to leave. But Tyree had a good team. A loyal staff. And the pull of home was overwhelming. He needed his son beside him. A few quiet hours.

And then tomorrow…

Well, tomorrow would come like it always did.

This time when Tyree stepped out of the employees-only area and into the large main room, Reece was behind the bar, relieving Eric. He nodded in acknowledgement, his expression sober and a just a little sympathetic, as Tyree headed toward the front.

He was almost to the door when Megan hurried up. "Hey," she said. "I don't want to hold you up, but could I grab you for a couple of minutes tomorrow before opening? I just want to go over some—"

"Sorry, sugar. I won't be back until Wednesday."

"Oh." He understood the surprise on her face. Tyree hardly ever took an entire day off. "Where are you—"

"Wednesday," he repeated, then walked away. And as he did, he heard Megan ask, "Where's he going? Out of town?"

And in the moment before the door to The Fix closed behind him, Tyree heard Reece's gentle reply. "He's going to go see his wife."

Chapter Two

TYREE WOKE to the sound of rain clattering on the metal roof of his Wilshire Wood house. He laid there, soaking up the sound and the memories. These were Teiko's favorite mornings, when the world seemed to close in around them, and they could stay warm and cozy in bed. She'd curl against him, her warm body convincing him that she was absolutely right about the magic of a rain-soaked dawn. They'd make love slowly, almost lazily, until a rising passion brought them both awake and to climax.

Yeah, definitely the best mornings. Hell, Eli had been conceived on just such a morning. And though Tyree felt the pang of loss—especially today of all days—he couldn't deny that the memory was sweet.

They hadn't had these kind of mornings in San Diego, but they'd moved to Texas in the summer and had both been charmed by the thunderstorms that so frequently filled the summer sky, cooling the wicked hot air to something bearable.

He stayed in bed a few moments longer, the thoughts of San Diego bringing up memories he hadn't expected today. Memories of Eva and the way they'd walked in the sun and splashed in the surf. He'd loved her, too, though their time together had been different. Shorter.

And though nothing could compare to the torment of losing Teiko to a slow, painful death from complications after a car accident, there was no denying that the break with Eva had been confusing and painful and so goddamn harsh. He hadn't understood it then, and he didn't understand it now.

All he knew was that Teiko had been the balm that healed those wounds. And he wished that he'd never seen that lithe young woman in The Fix. Because she'd put Eva in his head. And today of all days, Tyree didn't want to think of the first woman he'd loved.

Deliberately, he cast his thoughts back to when Eli was a toddler, and the way Tyree and Teiko would hold their son close between them during stormy weather, assuring him that everything would be fine. And then how they'd open the windows in the aftermath and let the cool air into the house, filling it with the scent of wet leaves and damp earth.

That was the best time to take a walk, and with Eli in his favorite blue rain boots, they'd explore the neighborhood, letting Eli stomp in the puddles and pick up the acorns, pinecones, and bits of bark and leaves that inevitably shook free after a storm.

"This is for you, babe," he whispered, some part of him wondering if she knew what he was thinking. If she understood how much he cherished those memories. Or if in some way that he couldn't comprehend, she still remembered, too.

With a sigh, he slid out of bed, then stumbled into the kitchen to get the coffee brewing. Once the machine was gurgling and the aroma of coffee began to fill the room, he turned back toward the hall, intending to go wake Eli. To his surprise, he met the boy coming in, already awake and fully dressed in pressed khaki slacks, a button down, and a sports coat.

"Looking spiffy, son," Tyree said, pride rising in his chest. They'd had their problems, especially right after they lost Teiko, but the boy was turning into one hell of a young man. And damned if Tyree couldn't see Teiko in the boy's looks, his mannerism, his smarts.

A petite Japanese woman, Teiko had made up for her small stature with a sharp mind and a big personality that Eli had inherited, along with his mother's eyes and a lighter skin tone than Tyree's deep burnished dark. And whereas Tyree was a large man, with the kind of broad shoulders that meant he had to have his suits tailored, Eli had a leaner build, inheriting only his father's height.

Looking at his son now, Tyree couldn't help but think that he and Teiko had made one damn good-looking kid. "You're gonna get that jacket soaked, you know. Your mom won't care if you're casual. I'm gonna put on jeans, a T-shirt, and a windbreaker myself."

Eli lifted a shoulder, then looked down at the floor. "I'm okay like this," he muttered, then lifted his head, his eyes looking guilty. "It's just that I need to go to the hospital today. Dr. Hanson's showing us all some stuff in the lab."

Another wave of pride swelled. Eli had recently been selected to participate in an exclusive internship at the nearby hospital, a position that both father and son considered a solid stepping stone toward Elijah's dream of going to medical school.

That pride, however, was laced with something cold and hollow. "You're not coming with me?" He glanced at the clock. Already six-fifteen. He needed to throw some clothes on if he wanted to get there on time.

"No," Eli said quickly. "I'm coming. It's just that after … I mean, I can't come back here with you like we usually do. Because of the work, I mean." He scratched his eyebrow with his forefinger, a nervous habit that Tyree recognized as one of his own. "I mean, that's what Mom would want, right?"

The tension drained from Tyree. "One hundred

percent. Why don't you pour us a couple of travel mugs of coffee while I go get dressed."

By the time he got back, Eli had the coffee ready to go and Tyree's car keys in his hand. The cemetery was on the other side of town, and traffic was a bear because of the weather and rush hour, but they made it with five minutes to spare.

They put down a tarp and knelt beside the marker —*Teiko Johnson, beloved wife and mother*. Beneath that, her birthday and the date she died. Seven years ago today. The rain had stopped, but the air was still damp, and the whole world seemed shrouded in gray.

"You okay?" Elijah asked. "I mean, you seem distracted somehow. More, I mean. More than usual for today."

Eva, Tyree thought, but he only nodded. Then he took his son's hand and said, "Quiet. It's time."

The cemetery spread out over the top of a small hill in Northwest Austin, and as Tyree and Eli looked to the east, the gray of the rain took on shimmers of gold and orange. Muted because of the clouds, but at the same time the colors seemed to dance in the air, reflected on the small drops of water that surrounded them.

They sat there, watching the sun rise above the horizon. As the colors changed. As the world came alive. And when the sunrise gave way to the full light of day, Tyree sat back on his heels and sighed. "Sunrise was your mom's favorite time of day."

"I know, Dad. You tell me every year. She liked it better than sunset because the sunset meant the end, and she loved beginnings."

Tyree blinked, his eyes suddenly damp and his throat thick. "I don't want you to forget."

"I know. I'm trying not to. I remember Christmas," he added. "She always got us up before dawn. And one day we walked on a beach in the dark, and then we made a sandcastle as the sun came up." He sighed. "But I've forgotten a lot."

"You were five on that beach trip. We'd gone to Port Aransas." He pressed his hand to his son's shoulder and squeezed. "And it's okay to forget," he said, even though he kicked himself hard with every one of his own lost memories. "Just hold tight to what is clear in your mind. And never forget that your mom loved you. That I love you."

Eli looked at him, his eyes seeming wiser than his sixteen years. "I know, Dad. I love you, too."

BACK HOME, Tyree spent the day as he did every year, the only difference being that today Eli wasn't with him. He made a big batch of jambalaya, downed a steady stream of bourbon, then settled onto the couch to watch *Blade*.

They'd seen the movie on their first date, even though he'd tried to do good by selecting what he considered a girl-friendly date movie, specifically, *How Stella Got Her Groove Back*.

But as soon as they'd arrived at the cineplex, Teiko had taken one look at the marquee, put her hands on her hips, and asked him why they weren't seeing *Blade* instead. Because, action. And, she'd added, Wesley Snipes was a bonus.

God, how he'd loved her.

He wasn't sure if he was luckier than most or cursed to have had that kind of passion. The kind of love that sunk into the marrow and made you part of the other person. That almost killed you, too, when you lost them.

He rubbed his eyebrow and sighed. The truth was, he would have withered away after Teiko died if it hadn't been for Elijah. That boy had been the wellspring of his strength.

And after Eva? After he came back from combat to learn that he'd lost her? That she truly, for certain, would never be his?

Well, in those dark days, it had been Teiko who saved him.

He drew a breath and let the memory wash over him. The heart-wrenching loss that had led him to Teiko.

He'd been twenty-two and on a short leave before shipping out when he'd met Eva in San Diego. Their romance had been hard and fast and intense, and the two of them had been absolutely inseparable.

He'd loved everything about her, from her strong personality to her quirky sense of humor to the soft little noises she made in bed. They'd walked along the beach holding hands, and even though they'd only known each a short time, they spent hours planning a future together. Plans that had sustained him when he traded the comfort and safety of Southern California for the heat and danger of the Persian Gulf.

But it had all been a lie. Not one of his letters was answered, and though he'd called her house, he'd never reached her.

When he returned to the states, he'd been stationed at Norfolk, and though he tried to forget her, he never quite managed. And finally, after years apart, he went back to San Diego and tried to track her down.

He'd found her. And not just her. He'd seen Eva with her husband, holding their little girl and laughing. And though he didn't have a clue how old the girl was, he knew enough to know that she wasn't a newborn. Which meant that Eva had barely even taken another breath before pushing Tyree's memory aside and landing in the arms of another man.

That knowledge—and the sight of how happy she looked holding her daughter—had ripped his heart in two.

He'd met Teiko hours later in the small cafe her parents owned. She'd been working as a waitress there on weekends. They'd talked, one thing led to another, and she'd completely stolen his heart. And healed it, too.

She'd been his rebound girl, no doubt about it. But she'd also saved him. And dear God, he'd been crazy in love with her.

The rattle of a key in the front door startled him from his thoughts, and he looked up to see Eli coming into the living room of the small house, every ounce of his attention focused on Tyree. "You okay? I know I should have stayed."

Tyree shook his head. "Hell, no. You had a job to do. And I'm fine."

Eli sniffed the air. "Jambalaya?"

"Nothing wrong with your nose, son."

"What are you going to make tomorrow?"

Tyree almost laughed, pleased the kid knew him so well. "I won't know until I make it, will I?" Every year after the anniversary of Teiko's death, Tyree lost himself in the kitchen, usually at The Fix. And usually he ended the day with a new menu item.

Eli laughed and settled onto the couch next to him. "I love you, Dad."

"I love you, too, boy." He put his arm and drew him close, sighing. He'd loved two women. He'd lost two. But he had his bar. He had his friends. He had his son.

It wasn't everything, but it was enough.

Chapter Three

EVA ANDERSON ADJUSTED the focus on her Nikon and took one final candid shot of the bride and groom sitting on a boulder and laughing, as friends and family circled around them, sharing the moment.

It was almost eight, the sky now full of light. But the couple had spoken their vows over two hours ago. They'd wanted a sunrise wedding at Desert Garden in Balboa Park, San Diego. And since they'd wanted it on the anniversary of their first date, Eva had found herself arriving with the small wedding party well before six a.m. on a Wednesday.

She'd come the day before to check out the specific location, and on the day of the wedding, she'd been able to integrate the charming cacti and other interesting plant life into the images. Now, as she started to pack her equipment away, she knew that she'd gotten some beautiful images. The couple, she was certain, would be thrilled.

"I can finish packing up if you want to go chat with the bride," Marianne said. Eva's part time assistant, Marianne also happened to be Eva's best friend. "And then, please God, can we go find a Starbucks?" She ran her fingers through her short, white-blonde hair as she yawned. "I need caffeine administered intravenously."

Eva laughed. "Sure." Frankly, she could use some caffeine herself.

She left Marianne to the task, then headed to where the bride, Jill, now stood with her mother. "The wedding was lovely," she said. "Thank you so much for trusting me with such important memories."

"Are you kidding?" Jill said. "I saw your pictures from Bill Landry's wedding and from my cousin Sarah's. I wouldn't have anyone else."

"That's so kind," Eva said, pleased to the bone, but hoping she sounded professional and not giddy. She'd quit her graphic design job five years ago to take a chance at her own photography business. Some days she still couldn't quite believe that she'd not only made a go of it, but that her little business was thriving and growing.

"We looked at your entire wedding portfolio online," Jill's mother added. "Such lovely work. You must really love weddings."

"Weddings and baby portraits are my favorite

things to shoot," Eva told them honestly. "They both have a little bit of the fairy tale in them."

"Happy endings," Jill's mother said, then stumbled a bit when her daughter hip-bumped her.

"New beginnings," Jill countered, with a gooey-eyed look toward her shiny new husband.

"Both true, I think," Eva added. She hadn't been merely telling the bride what she wanted to hear. She truly loved shooting weddings. And though she wasn't big on psychoanalyzing herself, she knew that one reason was that she mentally rewrote her own twisted fairy tale every time she heard those vows spoken.

Young and pregnant with a dead man's child, Eva had been roped by the father she'd adored and respected into marrying a man she didn't love. A nice enough man, sure, but not one she'd ever have a real future with, a real connection.

She thought of those years as she returned to her car where Marianne was loading the last of her lens cases and lighting kits. About the only good thing that came from her uninspired marriage to David was that Eva had finally grown a backbone. She'd filed for divorce on her twenty-fifth birthday, telling him that they both deserved more. He hadn't argued—hell, he'd almost seemed relieved—and once the divorce was final, he'd disappeared from her life.

Elena, thank goodness, had only been four. She'd missed the man she'd believed was her father, but the memories soon faded and Elena and Eva became a team. Single mom and darling daughter.

It hadn't been easy—especially since Eva's father had very loudly disapproved of her decision to divorce, and had backed up that disapproval by withdrawing all financial support. But they'd made it work, and Eva had come out stronger for it. Elena, too, she thought. Because how could a young woman grow up right if her closest role model was a woman who settled?

True, there was no man in her life, but that was okay. She'd focused on graphic design and learning photography, first as a hobby and then as a career. And she'd made sure that Elena heard lots of stories about her real father, Tyree, a Marine who'd gone to serve his country and had lost his life in the process. A hero.

Except it wasn't true.

Tyree hadn't died in the Persian Gulf like her father had told her. As far as Eva knew, he hadn't died at all.

But she'd believed her father's lie for over twenty years. Hell, he'd gone to his grave knowing he'd fed her a lie, and she'd only learned the truth a month ago when she'd finally decided to tackle the pile of boxes from his estate that were taking up much needed space in her studio's storage area.

She'd almost tossed the large envelope. It hadn't been addressed to her. All it had said was *Private*. She still didn't know what prompted her to open it. She still wasn't sure if knowing the truth was a blessing or a curse. But there was no going back now.

She'd used her forefinger to loosen the old glue on the envelope, then dumped out the contents. Five sealed letters in Tyree's scrawling handwriting, every single one sent from overseas, every one unopened. And she'd never before seen any of them.

And then, most insidious of all, she saw the single envelope without any writing on the outside. She'd opened it, then carefully unfolded the letter tucked inside. Elena had been sorting through another box, and though Eva didn't remember dropping to her knees, she knew that she had because Elena had cried out and hurried to her side.

"Mom?" Even now, Eva could hear the fear in her twenty-three-year-old daughter's voice. "Mom, what is it?"

In retrospect, maybe Eva shouldn't have told her. But in the moment, she'd simply held the note out. The single piece of paper on which her father had written out the truth, front and back, in his cramped, shaky handwriting. A truth revealed how he'd schemed and maneuvered after she'd tearfully confessed that she was pregnant. How he'd inter-cepted her mail.

How he'd flat out lied.

He'd told Elena that Tyree had died in combat. And because her father was a trusted military contractor with friends and connections at the highest levels, she knew he had access to the truth. And she'd believed him.

She'd been a fool.

He'd shifted the course of her life. All because he didn't want her marrying a poor man without any surviving relatives and only a high school education. A man who'd grown up in New Orleans, the son of a dirt poor Cajun mother and a father who'd worked as a janitor in Savannah before moving to Louisiana.

So he'd killed Tyree off—at least as far as Eva was concerned. And urged her into the arms of David Anderson, a man she didn't love and who didn't love her.

The reality had not only tainted her memory of her father, it had shaken her to the core.

As a young girl, Eva had felt like a princess. Though her mother had died in childbirth, her doting father had filled her with so much love and affection that she'd never felt sorry for herself. On the contrary, she'd felt cherished. Or she had until she'd learned that she was pregnant at nineteen. She'd told her father—her first mistake—and she'd been swept into a brand new story where she was no longer cherished. Instead, she was the soiled black sheep, forced to endure the worst.

In love with one man, forced to marry another. About the only good that came out of their union was

Elena. At least until Eva finally learned her own mind, grew a backbone, and filed for divorce.

Goddamn her father to hell.

And why he'd even written the truth was beyond her. Had he expected her to find it even though it wasn't addressed to her? Was it his way of confessing his sins?

She didn't know. She didn't care.

All she knew now was the truth—and the unpleasant fact that she had to tell a not-really-dead man that he had a daughter.

"Is this going to be one of those days where we only communicate telepathically?"

Marianne's words startled Eva from her thoughts and she turned to her friend. "Huh?"

Marianne nodded at the now packed rear of Eva's Honda Pilot. "We work in silence. We move as one. We are the Borg."

Eva rolled her eyes. "Sorry. Mind wandering."

"We've done six weddings since you found that stupid letter, and each one has sent you into a tailspin."

Eva's brows rose. "I am *not* in a tailspin. Distracted, maybe. But that's where I draw the line."

Marianne closed the hatch and leaned against the car. "Have you decided what to do? I mean, I know you're going to tell him, but have you decided how?"

Eva lifted a shoulder. "Not yet."

"You've known for a month." Marianne's voice was soft, yet chiding. "It's not going to get easier."

"I know. It's just—I don't know."

"Well, that's clear."

"Elena thinks I should just call him up. My romantic daughter thinks that he'll hear my voice, fly to San Diego, and we'll jump right in where we left off." Her half-smile was a little sad. "Except with a full-grown daughter instead of a bun in the oven."

"It might work out that way." Considering Marianne's usual brash snark, her voice was surprisingly gentle.

"Don't you start, too. Elena's still young enough to believe that love lasts forever. That people don't change. Get married. Have lives." He would have, she knew. Tyree would have a life. And while he deserved to know he had a daughter, she didn't want to mess up what he had. And, maybe, just maybe, she didn't want to stand outside his life and know that he was happy without her.

"Sure he has a life," Marianne said. "But you need to tell him."

"I know. I will."

"Sooner rather than later," Marianne said. Then hastily added, "That's only fair," when Eva narrowed her eyes at her friend.

"That's my plan, too. We don't have any shoots the rest of the week. I thought I'd see if I could track him down. Maybe see if I can get the military to give me his address."

"That might take awhile."

"Probably not that long." Eva dug her keys out of the pocket of the black jeans she always wore to shoot weddings. Coupled with a blouse and a jacket, it was just nice enough to blend, but durable enough that she could crawl around on the ground if that got her the killer shot.

She opened the driver's side door and climbed in, then waited for Marianne to get in on the passenger side.

"And a few more days won't matter. He's not exactly waiting by the phone pining for my call about a daughter he knows nothing about."

Besides, the more days that passed, the more she could work on controlling her nerves.

"Well, yeah, but…"

"But what?" Eva asked, her hand stalling on the key before firing up the ignition.

"Nothing."

"Oh, hell." Eva sat back, the key forgotten. She knew her friend well. Every expression. Every tone in her voice.

And she knew trouble.

"What's going on? And do not even try to pretend that I'm imagining things. Tell me."

Marianne licked her lips, her pale skin seeming paler against the cream colored leather. "Right.

Sure. Well, it's just—okay, you know how you always told Elena that a girl needed to go after what she wanted? To not hold back or let other people decide for her?"

"Yes." She heard the trepidation in her voice. It was a lesson she'd tried to impart after learning it herself and divorcing David. Now, she wondered if she was going to regret playing that particular parental card. "So?"

"It's just that she got tired of holding back."

Cold slithered up her spine. "What are you talking about? Elena? She's in Austin checking out the city and the University of Texas campus."

Elena had just graduated from UC San Diego, and she was taking a gap year while she decided where she wanted to apply to grad school. Her interest was in city planning, and the program in Austin appealed to her, so she'd decided to move there for the summer to see how she liked the town.

She saw the way Marianne looked at her, almost with pity. As if Eva was a foolish, foolish mother. "Hell. What aren't you telling me?"

"I'm sure she's all over the college thing. She raved about Austin and UT before she headed out."

"Uh-huh. And?"

"Yeah, um, about that *and*. I can't really tell you."

"Why not?"

"Because I'm your best friend."

Eva gaped, replayed the words in her mind, and

decided they still made no sense. "We really need to get you that caffeine. You're babbling."

Marianne sighed. "Do you remember when she was eight? Right after you divorced David? And you told me that she needed a confidante? An adult in her life who wasn't a parent. A woman she could ask questions to about boys or whatever?"

"I remember..."

"Well, I can't break the bond of confidence that *you* created."

"I was very specific. That bond doesn't apply if she's going to get hurt."

"Why would she?"

Eva glowered. "How would I know, since I don't even know what she's up to?"

Marianne only shrugged.

Determined, Eva reached into her purse and pulled out her phone.

"You're calling her?"

"No," Eva said. She'd realized that she'd never even tried to track Tyree down by normal means. She'd told herself she would ask the military because that gave her an out. A source for his location. No need for her to look on her own, right? She'd just contact the Marines after she got past the spate of weddings—today was the last on her books for three weeks—and returned from a much needed two-week vacation in Vancouver, where she was headed on Sunday.

So there'd been no need to pull up Google and search for Tyree Johnson—like she was doing right at that moment.

The results came up fast enough, and she gaped at the tiny screen on her phone.

"Austin. I knew it." She skimmed the text. "He owns a bar. Apparently they're doing some contest for a calendar because some local articles about it are the top three hits."

She looked up, realizing she was smiling. "One of the articles says that the bar—The Fix on Sixth—is known for its excellent food and cocktail menu, most of which are Tyree's invention." She remembered that he loved to cook, and had dreamed of opening a restaurant. Looked like he'd managed to make the life he wanted.

And he'd made it without her—that was something she needed to keep in mind. The fact that he had a life. Probably a wife and kids, too. A full, happy life.

A life that she and Elena were about to mess up.

And if Elena really was there to see him, then Eva needed to hightail it out to Austin. Because the one thing Eva absolutely didn't want was for the first—no, the only—man she'd ever loved to think she was a horrific bitch who purposefully kept the existence of his daughter hidden.

She exhaled a noisy breath. "Has she told him yet?"

Marianne's expression turned even more pitiful. "Come on, girlfriend. I told you. Confidential."

"Dammit, Marianne. Has. She. Told. Him?"

Her friend's shoulders drooped. "No. She chickened out. But she told me she's going to try again."

"When."

"Today."

"*Today*?" Holy shit. "I'll call the bar," she babbled. "Explain who I am. Maybe he's there. Maybe they'll give me his number."

Marianne tilted her head sideways, and Eva exhaled, then checked her watch.

"Or maybe I'm going to Austin."

Chapter Four

AS HIS SON HAD EXPECTED, Tyree spent Wednesday in the kitchen at The Fix. And by the time evening rolled around, and the place started to fill up with customers coming in for a drink and the Mr. April contest, Tyree had pretty much perfected a new recipe. He forced all the kitchen staff to taste—to unanimous approval—then tested the dish on a few of the after-work regulars, just to make sure his employees weren't blowing smoke up his ass.

Since the customers had given it the thumbs-up, too, Tyree called it a win and made a note to add it to the menu, just as soon as he figured out what to call it. Somehow, BBQ Bacon Chicken Pineapple Kebabs seemed a little too wordy.

Then again, maybe he'd run it by Jenna. She'd come up with a calendar contest. Maybe she could make a contest out of naming that dish, too.

Either way, by the time he'd tossed his chef's coat into the laundry and emerged into the main bar area, the place was hopping.

So busy in fact, that his bartender, Cameron, was looking a little crazed. Since Eric was on break, Tyree slid behind the bar himself, waving off Reece, who was hurrying in the same direction, obviously with the same plan.

"Thanks," Cam said, as he poured dirty martinis with blue cheese stuffed olives for two women in business suits. "I had it under control when I told Eric to take his break. Then we got slammed."

"No worries. And thanks for coming in tonight. We're short staffed." Not a good situation ever, but especially not on a Man of the Month night. And since Cam had recently been promoted to assistant weekend manager, this was one of his nights off.

"Honestly, it's no big deal. I already miss working alternating Wednesdays," Cam said. "The contest's the best show in town."

"You can say that again," Mina Silver said, slipping through the crowd and climbing gracefully onto a miraculously empty bar stool. She used the footrest for leverage, then rose up so she could lean over the bar and press a kiss to Cam's forehead. "Especially when Mr. March is on the stage."

She eyed him up and down. "Of course the part of Mr. March I really want to see is X-rated. Better wait until after hours."

Tyree forced back a grin as Cam shook his head in mock exasperation, then passed Mina a water.

"You laugh," Mina said, her green eyes sparkling as she blew a kiss toward Cam. "But we both know I'll get what I want."

Tyree held up his hands. "I hear nothing. I see nothing."

"A good policy," Cam said as he pointed to Mina. "And you're in for it later."

Mina batted her eyes innocently. "Can't wait."

Cam flashed a grin, then moved down the bar as the seat next to Mina opened up.

"Oh! Grab that for me!" Tyree glanced up from the draft he was pulling to see Amanda, a local real estate agent and another regular hurrying toward the now-empty stool that Mina was saving by putting her hand on the seat.

"Thanks. I'm desperate for a cocktail," Amanda said as she climbed up. "I need to be properly toasted in order to cheer Nolan on. I tried to convince Mom and Dad to come tonight, but they said they'd just rely on me to fill them in on the high points."

Tyree chuckled, remembering that Amanda and Nolan, a local radio personality, were step-siblings.

"You should talk to Brooke and Spencer," Mina said mischievously. "They might want you on camera. Giving the dish about a contestant. Could bring up ratings…"

"Could get me in the doghouse with my brother.

Besides, do you know the crap he could say about me on the radio? He knows way too many of my secrets."

"Tell me about it," Mina said. "My brother knows all of mine. Highly inconvenient."

"Aren't you working?" Tyree asked Mina.

She nodded, then held up her water and took a big gulp. "Just hydrating."

As she spoke, Megan came up, then tucked a long strand of hair behind her ear. "This looks like the best place to be," she said.

"Not anymore," Mina retorted. "I have to leave."

Megan laughed. "Even better if that means I get your stool."

Mina rolled her eyes. "No respect."

Megan waggled a finger, schoolteacher style. "We're supposed to be training for that 5K. You run this weekend with me and I'll show you respect."

With an impish grin, Mina glanced toward Cam. "I'm not usually out of bed that early on weekends…"

"Go," Cam said, laughing. "Before all *my* secrets are spread around this bar."

Mina winked at Tyree, then waved to the women before practically bouncing across the bar to where Brooke was discussing something about the reality show with one of the ever-present cameramen.

Megan climbed onto the vacated stool, and as she and Amanda shifted into gossip-mode, Tyree slipped into the crowd, talking with the regulars, shaking hands with the women who surrounded the stage, and then moving to the back to greet all the guys who were entered in the Mr. April contest.

He stayed there, watching from the back as the contest began, and cheering on each individual man as he strode toward the stage. With each contestant, the crowd got looser and Tyree noted that Tiffany and the other servers were hustling to fill the drink orders. Not bad, he thought, totaling a mental tab.

No doubt about it. Jenna had struck a genius moment when she'd conceived the contest. The crowd, the revenue. Hell, just the fun. On all counts, it was a top-notch idea.

So top-notch that he was a little surprised that his primary competition, Bodacious, hadn't swooped in to copy him. But so far, The Fix had the lock on local calendar contests. And when they printed the actual calendar and put it on sale in late October, that would be yet another revenue stream.

Hopefully all those streams would merge into river of enough money to keep the doors open come December.

Wistfully, he looked around the place, remembering the wreck it had been when he bought it. He'd refinished the long, oak bar himself, and Reece and Brent had helped with some of the other renovations. It was a great space. A space that he'd worked on with his bare hands. A space—and a business—that he loved. Filled with people he considered family.

He'd be damned if he'd let it go. If he'd walk away without a fight.

Not happening. Not this month. Not this year. Not ever.

With that thought ringing in his ears, he went back into the kitchen to check on the sanity of his cooks. On nights like this, things got a little crazy.

When he came back, the crowd was going wild and Nolan and the shy young woman Tyree had only met a few times—Shelby?—were locked in a clench.

His brows shot up and he turned to Reece, who was passing nearby. But all Reece did was shake his head, nod toward Nolan with a thumbs-up, and chuckle. Tyree laughed, too. The contest did seem to have the strangest effect on its participants.

Hell, maybe he should market the bar as a match-making venue.

A moment later, he saw that Nolan and Shelby were heading for the door. Since the winner hadn't yet been announced, Tyree considered calling them back. But he didn't. From the look on Nolan's face, wild horses couldn't keep him inside the bar.

He paused for a moment when Brent called his name, and he turned back to see his friend and partner signal for Tyree to reboot the security cameras. He flashed a thumbs-up and was about to head to the office to deal with that errand when caught a glimpse of the woman from Monday. The one who'd reminded him so much of Eva.

He froze. Simply froze. And as he watched her, a storm of bittersweet memories whipped around him, twisting up his insides and giving him no relief from the constant ache of long ago losses.

Resolutely, he forced himself to turn away. He needed to take care of the security system for Brent. More than that, he needed to get his head clear. He'd taken off yesterday to mourn his wife. Now that he was at work, he didn't need the distraction of an ex-girlfriend, too.

And yet the memories remained, and after he rebooted the system, he did the one thing that he knew he shouldn't. He sat down at his desk, opened his bottom drawer, and pulled out the battered cigar box. The one that he knew held a photo of Eva.

Slowly, he opened the box and pulled out a stack of faded photos. Elijah. Teiko. Birthday parties and Christmas scenes. And, yes, one of the funeral. Of Elijah in a suit, the nine-year-old boy trying so hard not to cry.

He forced himself to put them aside. To not get lost in the morass of memories he'd explored yesterday. Instead, he kept flipping, his eyes skimming over images of him and Charlie Walker, Reece's dad. And one of him with Reece's uncle, Vincent, just days before he'd been mortally wounded by enemy fire in Afghanistan, then died in Tyree's arms.

Another deep breath, and Tyree continued, finally finding the photograph he'd been looking for. Over twenty years old now, the colors had faded, so that Eva's dress looked pink rather than red, and the sky more gray than blue. But the love in her eyes was still there, and the face was still hers.

His heart twisted as he recalled their last weekend together in San Diego before he'd been shipped out. They'd known each other only two short weeks, but he'd been madly in love with her.

He'd learned soon enough that he'd been a fool.

With a sigh, he closed his eyes, his mind filled with the memory of both the women he'd loved. One he'd lost to death. The other had turned her back on him.

Both were gone.

There was a sharp knock on his doorframe, and he looked up to see a ghost.

He blinked.

No, not a ghost. That wasn't Eva. Of course it wasn't. But once again he was struck stupid by the resemblance.

"Mr. Johnson?" Her voice was lyrical yet strong and achingly familiar. "They said I could come back. I—you are Tyree Johnson, right?"

"That's me."

She drew in a breath, as if his words were a relief.

"And you lived in San Diego?"

A chill raced up his spine, and he thought of his grandmother, and the way she'd always say that a ghost had walked over his grave.

"I did. But that was a long time ago. So what can I do for you now, Miss…?"

"Anderson," she said. "Elena Anderson."

Elena. That had been his mother's name, too, and he looked at the girl more closely. "Who are you?" he asked, even though in his gut he already knew the answer.

"My mother is Eva Anderson. Well, she was Eva Wilson before. And I think that you're my father."

Chapter Five

TYREE SLUMPED BACK in his chair, all the air sucked from his lungs. He realized that he'd known what she was going to say. But anticipating her words and hearing them were two different matters.

And believing them was a third.

"I—" He cut himself off with a shake of his head. "Now, don't take this the wrong way, but that's just not so. I knew your mother, sure. But somehow you've gotten your wires crossed."

She drew in a breath, looked him in the eye, and said very simply, "no."

Then she stepped over the threshold into his office and sat down in one of his guest chairs. "It's true," she insisted. "You're my father."

Tyree's head was spinning. It wasn't true. It couldn't be true. But how was he supposed to convince this girl who so obviously believed she'd tracked down her daddy?

She was obviously Eva's daughter, that part he had no qualms with at all. The resemblance was striking enough to kick him hard in the gut, after all. But except for Elena's height and her skin tone, which was just a bit darker than Eva's, there was nothing about her appearance that seemed to come from him. More than that, he'd seen the man with her and Eva all those years ago. The black *couillon* who'd slid in and stolen Tyree's place. He'd been tall, too. And his skin quite a bit darker than Tyree's.

Then again, maybe the bastard had done him a favor. After all, what the hell would Tyree want with a woman who'd flip so quickly to another man and then keep the first man's child a secret from him?

Secret? No, she hadn't kept a secret from him. There was no secret.

There was no secret, he thought again, because this girl wasn't his daughter.

"Is this your family?" Her head was tilted as she looked at the frame with the photo of Elijah and Teiko. She reached for it, then turned it slightly on the desk so that she could see the image better.

"My wife," he said simply, silently begging Teiko to send him strength. "And my son."

"They're lovely." Her smile trembled a little, and she rubbed her eyebrow. "Look, I'm not here to—I mean, I'm not looking for anything. Honest. And maybe I shouldn't have burst in on you like I did. I should have called or written a letter. And so I get that I'm a shock. It's just that I found you and I wanted to meet you and——"

She cut herself off with a frown. "What is it?"

He realized he was staring at her fingers rubbing her brow, a familiar gesture he knew only too well.

He stood up, pushing out of his chair so hard that it rolled back and slammed into the wall. He bent over, hands pressed against the desktop as the room swam and he breathed hard, trying to steady himself.

He wanted to lash out at someone. Wanted to put his fist through the wall. Wanted do something, anything, to still the emotions that raged inside him.

Most of all, though, he wanted to not scare this girl. This lovely young woman who was an innocent in all of this.

His daughter.

Dear God, he had a daughter.

He closed his eyes and thought of Eli. *Teiko, I'm sorry. I thought it was just the three of us.*

"I really am sorry." Elena clasped her hands in her lap. "I honestly didn't mean to overwhelm you." He could see the nerves, but also the composure.

"You came in before," he said. "The other day, I mean."

She nodded, and a pretty smile flitted across her lips. "That was a baseline test."

"A what?"

Her chin lifted. "I was scared to come see you. I wanted to, obviously, but I was scared. So I did it in steps. Step one was getting through the door."

"Good thinking," he said, and an odd sense of pride filled him as he thought about this girl he barely knew and the fact that she was neither a fool nor a coward.

With a sigh, he sat back down. "Tell me about the man who raised you."

"The man?"

He didn't want to explain about flying out there and seeing her with her stepfather, so he said simply, "Anderson. Your last name's not Eva's, and it's not mine."

"Oh. Right. David and my mom got divorced when I was little. She doesn't talk about him much."

So Eva had gone from Tyree to some other guy. And pretty damn fast, too. Why? Because she wanted a father for her child? *He* was the damn father of her child. Why the hell hadn't she told him? Had Eva and this David asshole already been a couple even before Tyree and Eva had gone out? And then she'd run back into his arms?

The possibilities swirled in his head, each one pissing him off. He'd gone off to fight for his damn country, thinking that there was a woman waiting for him back home. A woman and the promise of a life together. Or at least the chance to explore that. To see if they fit together long term as well as they had for the short.

A lie.

Every memory that he'd clung to as bombs exploded around him—every memory that had soothed him to sleep, chasing away the nightmares of death and dismemberment—all of it had been a goddamn lie.

He wanted to shout. To lash out. To put his fist through the goddamn stone wall. But this poor child deserved none of that. She'd come looking for a father—for him—and no matter what else he might be, he wasn't asshole enough to take out his anger on her.

Slowly, deliberately, he forced himself to calm down.

"So what happened?" he asked. "Between your mom and this guy? David Anderson, right?"

"Right, and like I said, I was little. Only four. But from what she told me, they weren't compatible. As far as my life went, I was raised by a single mom. David didn't stay in the picture. Like, not at all."

"Not an easy life raising a kid alone." Eli had been older when Teiko had died, but still young. And it had been so hard that there'd been times when Tyree was afraid he was going to lose the kid for good to drugs or gangs or worse.

Eva and Elena at least had Eva's father to turn to.

Leroy Wilson had the resources to help his single daughter and granddaughter out.

"We did okay," Elena said. "I had a great childhood." She fidgeted a little, as if she was afraid she'd said something wrong. "I only mean that I didn't come here because my life is crap and I wanted you to fix it. My life's great. My mom's great. I really only came to meet you."

He sat back, made some sort of agreeable noise. The best he could manage, because at the moment he wasn't riding the *Eva's Great* train.

Elena looked down at the hands in her lap, her fingers twisting together. "She told me stories about you."

That surprised him. "About me?"

"Sure. She wanted me to know about my dad, right? She told me about you being a Marine. Said you were a hero."

Since he didn't know what to say to that, he said nothing.

"I wanted to know you so bad. And I missed you, too. Even though I'd never met you, I missed you. Does that make sense? Am I freaking you out? I'm sorry if I'm coming on too strong, but I—"

"It does make sense," he said gently as that little voice trilled in the back of his head. *A daughter. He had a daughter.*

And it did make sense. Because he'd missed her,

too, without even knowing she existed, he'd missed her.

"I know it's probably crazy, but I've wanted to know you my whole life," she said. "And so when I learned that you weren't dead, I just came. I really am sorry if I'm being pushy, but I—"

"*Wait.*" He leaned forward, his blood turning cold as he replayed her words in his head. "Who told you I was dead?"

"Well, I just knew. I mean, as I was growing up, and—"

"But who told you?" he repeated.

"I did."

He turned his head sharply toward the voice. Toward the woman standing in the doorway, a battered duffel bag hanging from one arm. A vision. A beauty.

A ghost.

His heart skipped a beat, and for a moment, time stopped as memory layered onto reality. She wore her hair short, just as she had back then. As Elena did now. And she had those same huge eyes, that same wide mouth, those same striking cheekbones.

She'd put on some weight, but it looked damn good on her. At nineteen, she'd been a skinny thing. Now, she was a woman, with curves in all the right places. The same, yet different. And so damned lovely it made his heart ache.

Once, he'd believed she was his woman. Now, he

didn't know what the hell to think other than that she'd betrayed him. Cut him more deeply than he could have ever imagined.

"I told her you'd died in combat," she was saying, and Tyree realized that the memory had crashed over him in the space of an instant.

A tear snaked down the side of her nose, and the lyrical voice he'd remembered so well sounded rough. "But you have to understand—"

"*Understand?*" He hadn't felt the rage building until it burst out of him, pushing him to his feet. All of his grief, his anger. All of his fears of being inferior. He'd known she was well-off. And he'd damn sure known that her father didn't approve of him. He'd thought it was real between them, but now—hell, now he knew that she'd just been having a fling. Screwing around with the soldier while she waited for her life to really begin.

"*Understand?*" he growled again. He saw Elena's eyes go wide and he tried to ramp it back, but it was as if seeing Eva had opened a floodgate, and two decades of buried pain had rushed back into him.

"You couldn't even tell her the truth?" he demanded as Eva stood frozen and mute, her eyes as wide as her daughter's.

He moved around his desk and took a step toward her. She stiffened, but she didn't move. Just stood tall and still and silent.

His anger spurred him on. "Had to kill me off.

Had to make me out to be some hero who'd died in combat saving the goddamn world? Couldn't give her one shred of truth about us."

He was only inches from her, so close he could hear her sharp intake of breath. He wanted her to answer him. He wanted a fight, and he remembered only too well how quick Eva's temper had been. "Or was there ever really an *us* at all?"

He didn't see it coming, but he damn sure felt it when her hard slap landed against his cheek, leaving it stinging.

Her eyes flashed with fury, and he could see a slew of words building up behind them. He waited, welcoming the tongue-lashing. The knockdown, dragout he craved.

But she didn't say a word. The slap notwithstanding, she'd learn to control her temper.

She turned slightly to face his desk, and he realized that she was looking at the photo of Teiko and Elijah. Then she turned back to him, her eyes flicking down to his wedding ring before she met his eyes, and in that moment, a feeling like shame crashed over him.

He pushed it back. He didn't have a goddamn thing to be ashamed of.

For a moment, she simply studied him. Then she shifted her attention to Elena. "You have some place to stay?"

The younger woman rolled her eyes. "No, Mom.

I've been here a week sleeping under bridges. Yes, of course I have a place. I'm watching a friend's apartment while he's doing summer studies at Cambridge."

Eva nodded, the gesture brisk and efficient. "Good. Marianne booked me a room at the Driskill. I'm going to go check in, and I'll text you my room number. You be there at nine o'clock tomorrow and we'll go have breakfast." She shot her daughter the kind of stern look that Tyree had seen generals use to quell the troops. "Do not be late."

"No, ma'am."

She nodded again, this time in satisfaction. Then, after shooting Tyree a look so cold it about froze his testicles, she turned and walked out of his office, her movements stiff, as if she was holding a storm inside of her.

That he understood. Because he damn sure was, too. And before he had the chance to either tamp it down or let it go, Elena was on her feet, her words and temper flying. Apparently that was a trait she'd inherited from both her parents.

"What the hell?" she bellowed. "I mean, seriously? What the ridiculous stupid hell do you think you're doing?"

He heard the light tap on the doorframe, then turned to see Brent. "Everything okay in here?" His eyes cut to Elena. "I heard shouting."

"We're fine," Tyree said, the words coming out sharp despite his best efforts to chill the fuck out.

Brent's attention shifted to Elena. "It's all good?"

She nodded. "It's fine. Thanks for checking."

Brent nodded slowly, and Tyree could practically see the questions and calculations zipping across his face. "I'm the one who sent Ms. Anderson back," he said. "Sorry if that was a bad call, but she said she was a friend of the family and Elena's mother."

Tyree's glance cut between Brent and Elena. "You two know each other?"

"We met in the bar earlier," Brent said.

"Huh." Tyree turned to Elena, lifted a brow in question, just the same as he did when he wanted Elijah to spill all.

She rolled her eyes. "I have a place to stay here, but I'm fond of eating, and I'll burn through my savings pretty quick. So I was asking about a job."

"Here?" Tyree asked.

"Well, yeah. But I didn't want to ask you because I thought it would be weird."

He ran a hand over his shaved head and sighed. If nothing else, at least the raging fire of his temper had burned itself out. "We can talk about that later," he said to Elena. To Brent he said, "It's all good. And shut the door on your way out."

To Tyree's irritation, Brent glanced toward Elena, as if requesting confirmation of the order. Did Tyree look or sound that rabid?

But it didn't matter. Elena nodded, and Brent backed out. And Tyree realized that he really was tight and stiff. But damned if he didn't have a good reason.

He'd lost a daughter.

No. Eva had stolen his daughter from him.

He thought of all the moments he'd shared with Eli through the years. The kind of moments he'd never experience with Elena. First steps. First birthdays. First day at school.

He looked at her, planning to tell her that he was sorry he'd missed that. Sorry that her mother had kept those moments from both of them.

He didn't expect—though he probably should have—the glint of steel in her eyes as she lashed right back into him again. "Just what the hell is wrong with you? My mother spent the last twenty-three years thinking you were dead, and you go off on her as if she was playing games?"

The anger Tyree understood. But the words weren't making any sense.

"Wait, hold on. Slow down." He frowned. "You said she told you I was dead. Hell, she said the same thing."

"Maybe you should have let her finish. She would have explained, you know. But I guess that didn't occur to you." Her voice was clipped, dripping with sarcasm.

"You explain." He sank back into his chair, suddenly unbelievably tired.

"She told me you were dead, because she believed

it. Because my grandfather was an asshole. All Mom ever said was how amazing you were. Like you'd been some fairy-tale prince who'd promised to come back and rescue her. Except you didn't come back because you didn't survive."

"Leroy told her I was dead?"

Elena nodded. "My grandfather. Yeah. And then she told me. She wanted to make sure I had a sense of you growing up. But I don't think I ever really believed it. That you were really dead, I mean."

He frowned. "Why not?"

A tiny smile tugged at her mouth. "Because then it wouldn't be a fairy tale, would it? If the prince gets eaten by the dragon? In a fairy tale, the prince has to slay the dragon."

"Are you sure I'm the prince in this story? Maybe I'm the dragon."

Her forehead crinkled. "Huh?"

He thought of Eva, and the way he went off on her. The cold, closed-off expression on her face before she'd walked away. "Yeah," he said softly. "I think maybe I'm the dragon in this one."

Chapter Six

EVA'S DUFFEL bag slapped against her side as she hurried through the bar and toward the exit door.

What had she been thinking? Seriously, what hellish demon with a twisted sense of humor had urged her to drop everything and jump on a plane? And why was she so ridiculously hurt that he didn't drop everything, swoop her into his arms and kiss her soundly?

She stopped midway out the door, the impact of the last thought hitting her. Because, dammit, it was true. Clearly, she was either losing her mind or reading too many romance novels, because somewhere deep inside she'd been nursing the insidious fantasy he'd pull her into his arms, tell her he'd missed her, and then cast a loving look at Elena and tell her what a good job she'd done raising their girl.

Idiot.

And not just because she'd pictured the scenario so damn wrong. No, she was an idiot for even fantasizing about him in the first place. After all, he had a life here. A bar he owned. A family he obviously loved if the picture on his desk and the ring on his finger was any indication.

And as for her, she had a thriving career back in San Diego. Austin was a diversion. She'd come to protect her daughter, not for herself. And the more firmly she kept that in her head, the better.

The light changed and she crossed Austin's busy Sixth Street. It was past ten p.m. on a Wednesday now, but still the street was hopping. She'd been here once before, during college, and she'd liked the town then. She hoped when she returned home from this trip, the memories wouldn't be tainted.

On the north side of the street, she turned left and walked the few short blocks to the stunning historic hotel that was tucked in among the modern buildings. She entered The Driskill through the main entrance on Brazos, nodding at the doorman who pulled open the glass door for her, then immediately relaxed. The place was stunning. A piece of late nineteenth century history with beautiful floors, tall ceilings, and every tiny detail seen to.

She mostly did portrait photography these days, but she itched to pull out her camera and take a few shots. Instead, she went to the front desk, got her key, and headed up to the room after begging a complimentary toothbrush to replace the one she'd forgotten in her haste.

On the way, she texted Elena her room number, and got a quick thumbs-up emoji in reply.

By the time she reached her room on the third floor, some of her anger had dissipated. After all, the man had been blindsided, whereas she'd known for a month that he was alive. She'd had time to think about him and to plan what to say. Granted, today's trip was a whirlwind— she'd barely had time to run home and toss a few things into her duffel before rushing to the airport—but the fact remained that she'd known what was coming. He hadn't.

So while his reaction had frustrated her—and, let's be honest, hurt her feelings—she kind of got it.

Her departure tonight would give him some time to cool off and adjust. Plus, Elena was there, and she could explain the whole convoluted tale about how they'd believed Tyree was dead—and why.

And it was best if that came from Elena, anyway. She was the one Tyree would want to see. Not Eva. Not when he already had a life with a wife and a son.

She sat on the edge of the bed and sighed, wishing she didn't care that he was married. That she hadn't seen the photo on the desk and the gold band on his finger.

But that was unfair, and she knew it. Time hadn't stood still for her; why on earth had she thought it would for him?

Except she hadn't thought it. She hadn't let herself think anything at all. But then she'd seen him and everything had flooded back. Memories, hopes, dreams, regrets.

She'd walked into his office and seen him. His heavy brow softened by the kindest eyes she'd ever seen. His broad shoulders. The strong arms that had held her so tight, keeping her safe and warm. His big hands, so gentle on her bare skin. And that wide, delicious mouth that had done such decadent things to her body.

In her mind, he'd come to her. Held her. Closed his mouth over hers, and the world had fallen away.

In reality, everything had blown up, including her fantasies.

"You're a fool, Eva Anderson. And you need to get over yourself."

True enough, and to punctuate the thought she got undressed, found the fluffy hotel bathrobe in the closet, and settled down on the bed to find the stupidest, most mundane program she could. She'd let the power of bad television drain her mind and tomorrow when she saw Tyree again, they could both act like adults.

Adults who'd moved on with their lives.

Because that, of course, was who and what they were.

She was just dozing off to a rerun of an eighties

sitcom when a sharp rap at her door jolted her back to consciousness.

Elena.

Still half-asleep, she rolled out of bed, tiny prickles of trepidation urging her to hurry. Why on earth had she told Elena to come tomorrow? She should have insisted the girl come tonight. Anytime tonight. After all, her daughter had just met her father for the first time; of course she needed her mom now.

With a quick tug to tighten her robe, she hurried to the door, and yanked it open.

Then she froze. She just simply froze.

Because it wasn't Elena standing there. It was Tyree.

"Oh," she said, then wished she could surreptitiously pound her head against a wall. "I wasn't expecting you."

Also another piece of conversational brilliance. Yeah, she was doing great tonight.

Those kind eyes she'd seen in her fantasy were focused intently on her—on *all* of her—and she was suddenly acutely aware of exactly how much nothing she had on under her robe.

She pulled it even tighter, and he cleared his throat, then shifted his eyes to her face. She blushed, and at the same time she desperately wished she'd known he was coming. The bathrobe was hardly flattering. If anything it accentuated the twenty pounds she'd put on over the years, most of which had gone straight to her hips.

"I'm sorry to show up unannounced," he said in that low voice that flowed like honey. "I thought you wouldn't see me if I called first."

A hint of a smile softened his words, but the truth was, he was right; she absolutely wouldn't have.

She conjured a smile of her own, to let him know it was okay. Especially since she knew perfectly well who his cohort in crime had been. The Driskill was far too classy a hotel to randomly give out a guest's room number.

"Can I come in?"

She glanced down at her robe, then over her shoulder at the mussed bed. "That would be no."

"I promise not to ravage you," he said, and though it was clear he meant the words innocently, the way they teased her senses was anything but. Her nipples peaked and her inner thighs tingled, and she wanted to kick herself for reacting like a hormonal teenager, but a year-long dry spell would do that to a woman.

"Not to challenge your integrity, but I don't think it's a good idea. Besides, what would your wife think?"

The moment the words were out, she knew she'd made a mistake. His smile faded and a shadow crossed his face, filling those wonderful eyes with sorrow.

"I'm so sorry, I didn't mean—"

"She passed away. Seven years ago."

Eva swallowed, then had to forcibly fight the urge to invite him in after all so that she could comfort him. "I saw the picture. Your ring. I just assumed…"

He looked down at his hand. "I didn't even realize."

She cleared her throat. His loss hung between them, almost palpable. And for one horrible, hateful moment, Eva felt a stab of jealousy for the dead woman.

What the devil was wrong with her?

She hadn't been around Tyree for two decades. What right did she have to insert herself into his life in any way, even in her own fantasies?

This time, Tyree cleared his throat. "Listen, I get the hesitancy to let me into your room. But I would like to talk. The bar downstairs is quiet. Have a drink with me? It's neutral ground."

She glanced down at her robe. "I'm not exactly dressed for it."

"I bet there's something stunning in that duffel bag of yours."

She laughed out loud at that. "Yeah, I crammed some fabulous designer wear into that thing." She drew in a breath. "Listen, thanks for handling it well with Elena."

He cocked his head as he grinned, the combination so familiar that her stomach did a flip-flop. "How do you know I did?"

"She wouldn't have given you my room number if you'd been an ass."

"I was an ass," he said. "But then I backtracked."

This time she bit back the laugh before an unattractive snort emerged. "Glad to hear it." She licked her lips as she gathered her words, because it was important she got it right. And, frankly, it was hard to concentrate with him so close and her so naked under the robe.

"The thing is," she began, "I know Elena's a grown woman now, but she has this image of you. You're practically a superhero. A romantic figure who went off to battle and was killed in action. You were her daddy, and everything she heard filtered through the lens of awesomeness."

"And for you?"

Her smile came easily. "I felt the same. But this isn't about me. I want you to understand her. She's smart, and she goes after what she wants. But there's still a young girl inside her who believes in fairy tale endings. And you coming back from the dead is just going to cement that."

She wiped her palms on the robe, then nodded at a couple who walked past the room and the open door, their heads turned just enough to make clear they were curious about the conversation on the threshold.

When they were gone, she continued. "I'm rambling, but the point is that whether you wanted her or not, she's yours. You don't have to love her. You don't have to want her. But please don't hurt her."

Something hard flickered on his face. "Do you really think I would?"

"Twenty years ago, no. Now?" She lifted a shoulder. "The truth is I don't know you at all."

"Then get to know me again. Come downstairs. Give me a chance to apologize for being an ass earlier. And let me convince you that I won't hurt our daughter."

Our daughter.

The words curled around her, tempting her. But at the same time reminding her of her priorities. Elena might be 23, but where finding her daddy was concerned, she was still a little girl. Hell, she'd always be Eva's little girl, and that came first. That had to come first.

And, honestly, Tyree needed time, too.

Not that she expected that a drink in the bar would lead to a wild tryst. She didn't. As attracted to him as she might still be, there were too many years under the bridge.

More than that, though, right now she needed to behave like a grownup, not like the nineteen-year-old she used to be, floating a foot off the ground because she was so full of love.

"Maybe tomorrow," she said.

"Tomorrow?" He did that delicious head tilt

again, his eyes narrowing as he looked at her. "Is that a promise?"

But she just smiled. "Goodnight, Tyree," she said, then closed the door.

Sometimes it really sucked to be a grownup.

Chapter Seven

AFTER EVA SHUT HIM DOWN, Tyree knew he should head back to The Fix and put in a few more hours. He wasn't officially on the schedule tonight—Reece was the manager in charge through the rest of the week—but there was always work to be done, and most nights Tyree was eager to do it.

Not tonight though. Tonight, he felt off.

Tonight, he just wanted to wander.

It had been a long time since he'd done that, actually. Just strolled along Sixth Street and checked out the restaurants, the bars, the theaters. Things had changed since he'd first moved to Austin, but not so much he didn't recognize the place. Sixth Street was always humming, and it was easy to get lost in the light and the noise, the smell and the rhythm.

Right then, he wanted to get lost. Wanted the rhythm of the street to wash away the strange disappointment that was flowing through him. He shouldn't care so much that Eva had turned him down. He shouldn't want so much to sit with her across a table and watch her sip whiskey.

She liked it neat, he remembered. She'd only been nineteen, but she'd drunk her whiskey neat. Her father, she'd told him, had insisted she learn how to drink real liquor. No froufrou cocktails for her. Not on her Daddy's watch.

He wondered what she'd think of his menu at The Fix. Of the fun cocktails like the Sparkling Pineapple and the Fizzy Watermelon. Hell, maybe he'd fix her and Elena a pitcher of his special sangria. Or some Candy Corn Jell-O Shots. Then they could see if Elena was more Eva's daughter or his.

Thoughts of Eva and Elena filled his head as he walked east on Sixth, not stopping until he'd almost reached the highway. He crossed the street, his stomach growling when he breathed in the scent of yeast as he passed the Easy Tiger Bake Shop.

As he got closer to The Fix, he realized that he'd had a destination in mind all along. Not his own place —his competition.

Bodacious.

There were other bars in the area, of course. And technically all of them competed. But Bodacious was particularly vile. A corporate bar with franchises all over the country, Bodacious was the kind of place that hired managers who made it their mission to suck the marrow from local establishments. And even in a town like Austin that thrived on the concept of local, a place like Bodacious with its deep pockets could reshape the face of a neighborhood.

He paused in front of the glass and chrome entrance with the faux car parts and the scantily clad mannequins. Inside, the real waitresses wore even less. Shorts so short they were practically bikini bottoms. And T-shirts cut off so that the red lace of the servers' matching bras was impossible to miss.

The hostess stand was unmanned, and he took a menu, then studied it, wrinkling his nose at the unimpressive array of drinks that he knew were more water than liquor.

And yet this was the place that was grabbing his customers.

Honestly, he wouldn't believe it. Except that he saw a few of his former regulars over in the corner, huddled over a bucket of fries, dollar beers in front of them, and ESPN blaring from the television mounted just a few feet away.

"We give them what they want *all* the time," Steven Kane said, seeming to materialize at Tyree's side. Then again, Tyree had always thought that Kane was a vampire, sucking the life out of the community. So maybe he had formed out of dust and smoke.

"You give them girls in next to nothing and lame drinks."

Steven grinned. "Like I said. Besides, you're doing the skimpy. Shirtless men on stage? Sounds like exploitation to me."

"Give it a rest, Kane."

"Hey, I'm not criticizing. Who knows? Maybe we'll start doing the same thing. Competition's the American way, right?"

Tyree turned away, really not wanting to look at Kane any more than he had to. As he did, he caught sight of a familiar face. "Is that your idea of competition?" he asked, nodding toward Aly. "Going into my place and poaching my employees."

"I pay a living wage. Most people find that hard to turn down."

"I can't keep you from talking to them, but if I hear that you're talking to them inside The Fix, you and I are going to have some private words in an alley. Are we understanding each other?"

Steven held up his hands. "Why so angry? Come on, Johnson. Let me buy you a drink. You need to relax."

"Just stay the fuck out of my way and out of my bar. Are we clear?"

"I need to go see about a guest. But feel free to stay. Have a drink. I recommend the Pinolicious Punch. Fabulous."

And then he scurried away like the little rat he was. *Pinolicious his ass.* A complete rip-off of Tyree's Pinot Punch, he was damn sure of it.

He was still seething when Aly came over. "Hi," she said, looking small and contrite and very awkward. "I'm really sorry. I just needed the extra money. And the tips. I should have told you first. I was gonna try to cover both jobs for a few weeks. But I don't think I can handle it."

"It's okay," he assured her. "I get it."

The truth was, it was his own damn fault. Tiffany had warned him that Steven was courting Aly, and Tyree hadn't wanted to lose the excellent waitress he'd trained as a bartender. But he hadn't done a thing to keep her. Not yet, anyway. And now he really had no one to blame but himself.

He started to go, then paused and turned back to the girl. "The Pinolicious Punch. Is it—"

"Almost," she said. "But not really. And not as good. Apples instead of peaches. And no Schnapps. Kane says that takes the base price up too much."

"Thanks," he said, feeling better. Because that really did sound like one nasty-ass drink.

Still, the frustration over losing Aly ate at him, and he made a mental note to look over payroll. They always needed good bartenders. Maybe The Fix could justify hiring her back at a higher pay rate.

Work and family battled it out in his head as he reached his car, then drove the short distance to his house. But as soon as he stepped inside, family won. It always did when he came home, because here was where Eli was the priority.

But it wasn't just Eli now, was it? Sure, the boy was his only minor child. The only child for whom he was legally responsible. But that wasn't the issue. Elena was his. She was family.

And there were decisions to be made.

Exhaustion swept over him, and though he wanted to fall face down in his bed, he moved quietly through the house to Eli's room, pushed open the door, and watched his sleeping son.

He didn't know how long he stood there, but just seeing the boy steadied him, and soon enough he moved to his own bedroom. He was exhausted. Tired and drained and desperate for sleep. But sleep wouldn't come, and after an hour he ended up in the living room on the couch in his boxers and a T-shirt with the TV on. Not that he was paying attention to the show.

No, his mind was back on Eva.

At the time he'd asked her to go downstairs for a drink, he hadn't been entirely sure what he wanted her answer to be. But apparently he'd been hoping for a *yes*, because her *no* was damn sure bothering him.

Why?

For a brief moment he imagined the feel of her naked body pressed against his, all soft and curvy and *his*. But no. That wasn't what he wanted. *It wasn't.*

He didn't want or need the complication of sex. All he wanted was for Eva to tell him about Elena.

About the years that he missed. Her babyhood. Her first steps. Her friends, her dreams.

He needed Eva to be a scribe for him, writing the missing memories of his daughter on his mind.

That was it. That was all it was.

Easy. Simple.

And now that he knew, he should be able to sleep.

Yawning, he returned to his bedroom, then slipped between the cool sheets. He closed his eyes, remembering the way Teiko's petite body tucked against his. Nothing like Eva's long limbs. With a flash of memory, he recalled that Eva used to kick him in bed. One time, she'd even got him in the balls. Restless leg, she'd called it.

How the hell had he forgotten that?

He opened his eyes, then looked at the near-empty bed that suddenly seemed too full.

With a sigh, he once again slid out of bed. This time, he took his pillow with him to the living room, then settled down on the couch to sleep.

He didn't know how long it took before he slipped under, but when he clawed his way back up to consciousness, the room was full of light, and his son was standing over him.

"So what's up with you?" Eli demanded.

Tyree rubbed his head as he sat up. He blinked, trying to clear the sleep from his eyes. "Just couldn't settle last night."

"No, I mean, you watched me sleep. What was that about?"

"You were awake?"

"Not really. You know where you're like half in a dream? It was weird."

"Just wanted to check on my boy."

Eli frowned, like Tyree was a crazy person, but shrugged. "So why the couch?" He looked at Tyree's pillow, making clear that he wasn't going to fall for any bullshit about accidentally falling asleep there.

But since Tyree couldn't exactly tell his son that he'd been feeling strange—maybe even guilty—about the bed that he'd shared with Eli's mother, Tyree just shrugged.

He couldn't tell him that, but he had to tell him something.

With a sigh, he pushed up off the couch. "Come on. Let's go make French toast."

Eli's eyes actually went wide. "Oh, God. Am I in trouble?"

Tyree chuckled as he looked over his shoulder at the kid. "What? No. Why?"

"We only have French toast when we need to have a *talk*. I know about sex, Dad. I'm all good."

Tyree grimaced. "Do you need to get to the hospital this morning?"

"Nope. I'm staying over at Jeremy's lake house until Saturday, remember? It's got this amazing room with a big ass TV, and we're going to kick back and play Overwatch."

"That video game?" Tyree asked, and then continued at Eli's nod, "Sounds like one hell of a good time. I won't keep you long. And you're not in trouble."

"Okay," Eli said, but he sounded dubious. "I'll get out the bread."

Apparently they'd had quite a few talks over the years because Eli pitched in with the cooking without any instruction from Tyree, and soon enough breakfast was on the table. Despite his best intentions, Tyree hadn't managed to bring up Eva or Elena. But as soon as he sat down, he knew that he had to. Eli was his boy, and he deserved to know.

"You can just spit it out, you know," Eli said, a sticky piece of French toast on the end of his fork. "Unless you were lying and I really am in trouble, in which case take all the time you want."

Good God, was it any wonder he loved the kid?

"I dated a woman before I met your mom," Tyree said.

"Well, yeah. I mean, I kinda assumed."

"She's in town."

"That's totally cool. I mean, I get the whole sex thing. It's been like a long time for you, huh, Dad?"

Tyree almost spit out the orange juice he'd just sipped to wet his damn mouth.

"Christ, Eli."

"What?" He stirred a piece of bread in a pool of syrup. "I thought you were going to tell me you wanted to see the lady."

A knot twisted in Tyree's stomach, because maybe he did. But that wasn't something he needed to think about now.

He took a deep breath. "I just found out she has a daughter."

Eli's eyes never left his face. "Oh. Oh, wow." The boy leaned back, considering that. "Okay."

"Okay?"

"Well, like, she's yours right? 'Cause why tell me?"

"Yeah." He felt pride swell as he thought about Elena, a remarkable young woman for whom he'd had the tiniest bit of responsibility in creating. "Yeah, she's mine."

"Like I said, okay."

"I'd like to get to know her," Tyree added. "And I —I hope you're okay with that. That you'll get to know her, too."

Eli finished off his French toast. "Well, yeah. 'Course I am. She's your kid. And she's my sister."

"Half-sister."

"Same thing. How old is she? Is her dad okay with all this?"

"She's twenty-three, and he's not in the picture. Her mother divorced the man she married after me a long time ago. Elena doesn't even really remember him."

"Elena. Okay. Well, yeah. It's all cool, Dad." He pushed back. "Can I go to Jeremy's now?"

Tyree studied his son, looking for signs that this was the kid's way of escaping, but all he saw was a boy eager to go play his favorite video game.

"You're okay? You don't need to talk?"

"About what?" He looked at Tyree's face, then exhaled. "Come on, Dad. You remember Raptor, right?"

Tyree fought back a shudder as he thought of the gangbanger and the two years after Teiko's death when Eli had come so close to going off the rails. "Yeah, I remember him."

"He was a screw-up, Dad. I know that. I'm cool. Don't look so freaked. I'm just making a point."

"Which is?"

"His dad basically told him to fuck—I mean shove off. And it messed with him. I'm not saying that's the reason Raptor turned out like that, but I figure it got under his skin." He lifted a shoulder. "But his dad was a real a-hole, and you're not. So, of course you're going to want to get to know her. Same goes for me if she's my sister. It's kind of a no-brainer."

"Huh." Tyree leaned back in his chair.

"What?"

"You're pretty mature for a sixteen-year-old."

"Yeah?" His face lit up. "Remember that when I ask for a car."

Chapter Eight

"SO YOU'RE REALLY NOT mad that I gave him your room number?" Elena asked as they dug into waffles in the 1886 Cafe at The Driskill.

"You really shouldn't have. A room number? Elena, you should know better."

Her daughter rolled her eyes. "It's not like I gave it to just any guy on the street. I mean, he's my father. So it's not like the sight of you in a room with a bed will weird him out. I mean, exhibit A." She pointed to herself. "There was sex at some point."

Eva rubbed her temple. "Sometimes the inner workings of your mind baffle me."

"I am a mystery," Elena said.

"And you still shouldn't have told him the room number."

Elena rolled her eyes. "Better than your phone number. I mean, you're only going to be in the room for a few days. Give him your phone number and he can hound you forever. Even if you decide you don't want to talk to him anymore."

Eva frowned, then lifted her hand to signal for more coffee. "He's your father. Of course I'd talk to him if he wanted."

"You didn't last night."

Eva leaned back in her chair as the server refilled her mug. "And there it is."

"What?"

"That sharp mind that earned you *summa cum laude*."

Her daughter rolled her eyes. "I come from good genetic stock."

"Uh-huh. Way to butter me up."

"What makes you think I was talking about you?"

Eva laughed. "Fair enough." She pushed back her empty plate. "Shall I get the check? I want to see your apartment."

"Sure. Just please, *please*, Mom, keep in mind that it's not my place. So you can't dive in and redecorate."

"I'm not interested in the paint job. I want to see the area and the building. I want to know that my baby's safe."

Elena rolled her eyes. "It's in the parental DNA or something."

"What is?"

"Tyree hardly even knows me, and he said the

same thing last night. He wanted me to text Gordon and see if it's okay for me to change the locks, because who knows how many guy friends Gordon's given a key, too."

"He said that? It's a good point."

"Yeah, I thought so, too. So I texted Gordon this morning and he's cool with changing out the locks."

"You can use my credit card for the locksmith," Elena said, once again relieved to know that her daughter had access to a high-limit credit card. And, more importantly, was responsible enough not to use it for makeup and cocktails.

"It's all good. I texted Tyree right after. He said we could drive out to the apartment after my meeting at the bar and he'd change them for me."

"Meeting?"

She lifted a shoulder. "I was talking with the security guy yesterday—Brent—and he said that I should talk to Reece or Jenna. They might have a job for me."

"Oh." Eva leaned back in her chair. "Well, that's excellent. And it just makes me more convinced that I'm not making a huge mistake."

"A mistake?"

"Going back home."

Elena leaned back, then forward, then back again. "Wait. What? You're leaving?"

"You have a place to live, and you found your father and, most likely a job. Even if you don't end up working at The Fix, it's clear he'll help you out. And you should have the chance to get to know him."

"But—"

"So I'm going to go back to San Diego tomorrow."

"Tomorrow! Why?"

"Because tomorrow's Friday and I leave on Sunday for Vancouver, remember?"

"Yeah, but…"

"I'll come back after my vacation and check on you." She leaned across the table and took her daughter's hand. "You'll be fine."

"Go back on Saturday."

Eva felt a tug at her heart. In so many ways Elena was a grown woman, but being out on her own and away from her home town had brought out the little girl who needed her mom. "I can't do that, baby girl. That only gives me one day to get everything packed and ready before my vacation."

And, dammit, it was hard being around him. Wanting what she couldn't have. What had passed her by.

She said none of that aloud, and yet from the way Elena was studying her, Eva felt like she might as well have.

"What happened to my mother?" she asked.

"What do you mean?"

Elena put her elbows on the table and leaned over her sticky waffle plate. "What happened to the woman who told me to go after what I want? Seriously, Mom. Just make a move."

The thought of making a move on Tyree filled Eva with a combination of awkward dread, delicious anticipation, and utter terror. "You're imagining things. I wanted your father a long, long time ago. Now all I want is for you to get to know him."

"You might want to say that again. It was hard to understand with your nose growing so fast while you talked."

Eva rolled her eyes. Honestly, her daughter was too damn smart.

And, yes, she did still want him. But she was afraid that he didn't want her. Or that even if he did, the initial spark would fizzle, and they'd stumble along in some anorexic relationship that would sap the joy out of the memories of all their good times.

Better to cling to the good than risk destroying it completely.

"Fine," Elena said. "Forget Tyree. But don't abandon your only daughter."

At Eva's amused shake of her head, Elena plowed on.

"Please, Mom. Just stay one more day. You always throw half your closet into a bag, so it's not like packing takes time."

"I do not!" Eva protested, even though she absolutely did.

"I wanted us to spend some time out here. Go to

the Hill Country. Tour all those wineries. Aunt Marianne even gave me a present so we could go in style."

"She did? When did you talk to Marianne?"

"Last night," Elena said. "I caught her up."

Eva nodded. That explained the texts that had been waiting for her when she'd checked her phone this morning.

Well?

And then ten minutes later…

Hello?

And then forty-five after that…

Fine. Tell me when it suits you. Just TELL ME.

Eva wasn't entirely sure what she was supposed to be telling, since apparently Elena had already revealed all. But she'd give her friend a call later anyway. Besides, she had to ask her to change the return flight.

"So you'll stay?" Elena asked, the question more of a statement.

"I haven't said so yet."

Elena waved it off. "It's all over your face. This is amazing. We can go tour some wineries. Shop. Hang out. It'll be stellar."

"Yes," Elena said, then took her daughter's hand. "It will."

Chapter Nine

TYREE COULD SAY one thing for his daughter—she was a charmer.

When he walked into The Fix on Thursday afternoon, there were only a few customers at scattered tables. But half his staff was gathered around Elena at the bar as she sipped from a line-up of drinks and laughed at something Reece was saying.

"Hey!" She looked up and flashed him a smile so broad she seemed lit from the inside. "I'm learning the menu. The better to recommend a favorite to customers. So far, I'm pretty sold on the Jalapeño Margaritas."

"I can see I'm not going to have any help with those locks. By the time we get to your apartment, you'll be seeing two doorknobs."

She blinked. "There are two knobs. One on each side of the door."

Behind the bar, Cam laughed. "She has you there."

"Seriously, I'm only tasting. Everything's great."

"Tiffany's in the back putting together a sampler tray of appetizers, too," Jenna added. "We figured Elena was right. If she's going to work here, she needs to know the score. Oh! And a T-shirt." She cocked her head, silently urging Elena to follow. "Let's go get you one from the back while we wait for the food."

Elena flashed a brilliant smile at Tyree, then followed. As soon as she was out of earshot, he turned to Reece. "So it's settled? She's working here?"

"For the summer, anyway."

"Good," Tyree said.

"Guess that makes her one of the family." Reece's eyes were on Tyree. Not hard, but knowing.

Tyree felt a quick twinge of guilt. Everything had happened so quickly he hadn't told his friends about Eva or Elena. Clearly, though, they'd found out.

"Sorry, man," he said, and got an answering smile from Reece.

"We're all good. She's great, and just so you know, she's not the one who told us. Brent flat-out asked her. I guess he caught part of your discussion with her mother yesterday."

"If by *discussion* you mean my off-the-rails rant, yeah, he did."

"Well, Elena's great," Reece said. "And she seems happy to be working here." He frowned. "Listen, it's okay with you, isn't it? Honestly, I should have asked you first, but that girl's a force of nature."

He rubbed his hand over his shaved head, looking more than a little overwhelmed. "She came in, we started chatting, and the next thing I knew, I'd put her on payroll."

Tyree chuckled. "She takes after her mom."

"That so? And how does Mom fit into this new picture?"

Tyree drew in a breath. Of everyone at The Fix, Reece knew him the best. Reece's dad had looked after Tyree when he was green and in combat. And years later, Tyree had held Reece's uncle in his arms as he'd bled out, trying to offer some comfort to the mortally wounded man.

So yeah, he and Reece had a bond. And maybe it was that bond that made him tell the truth. Or maybe it was just the need to talk to another man. To say it out loud. "I don't know," he admitted. "I want her here, Reece. I want to get to know her again. But—" He shook his head. "I thought about her last night. She was right there in my head as I lay in my bed. *Our* bed." He drew in a breath. "I had to move to the goddamn couch."

Reece nodded thoughtfully. "It's hard to move on."

The words were obvious, but they helped. Just acknowledging that it was hard helped, and Tyree sighed. "Hell, yeah, it is."

"Take it slow. See what happens. Maybe nothing will. Or who knows? Either way, you're not cheating. And you're not staining her memory."

"I know," Tyree said. But those were just words. In his heart, he didn't really know at all.

Behind them, he heard Jenna's bright, "Ta-da!"

He turned to see his baby girl filling out one of the black *The Fix on Sixth* T-shirts.

"Looks good, huh?" Elena said.

"Looks great," Tyree told her, as she came back over, then twirled in front of the bar. She grabbed one of the drinks, then handed another to Jenna for a toast. Jenna, he noticed, didn't drink hers, and after a few moments surreptitiously traded it for a sparkling water.

"I did a little bartending in San Diego," Elena said. "Reece said you're short on servers and bartenders. So I can do whichever you need." She grinned, then batted her eyes. "I'm so much more than just the boss's daughter."

They all laughed, but then Jenna said, "Too bad you're not a photographer, too."

"Oh." Elena's mouth curved down. "I'm not bad. Mom's had me behind a camera since I was six. Why?"

"What's Eva got to do with it?" Tyree asked.

"That's what she does. You didn't know?"

"I didn't, no." He realized he was smiling. "Good for her."

Elena's brows went up, obviously in confusion.

"She used to screw around with this crappy point and shoot thing, but she took some great pictures with it. I'm no expert, but I thought they were amazing. So I bought her a present before I shipped out. A Nikon. I don't remember the model. And I told her to document the days for me."

"You gave that to her? She still uses it."

He blinked. "Seriously?"

Elena nodded. "Well, she has new lenses, of course. But she told me it had sentimental value." She grinned. "She never told me it was from you, though. Probably afraid I'd beg to have my daddy's camera. And as for the days, I guess she listened to you, because she takes a picture every day no matter what."

"Does she?" His heart squeezed so tight he had to reach for the bar to steady himself. "And she really kept it. The camera?"

Elena lifted a shoulder. "Why not? She loved you."

He turned away, faking a cough so that neither she nor the rest would see the tears that had welled in his eyes.

When he turned back, Jenna was studying Elena. "Do you do portrait work? How about shots of food?" She explained about the contest, the calendar, and the cookbook.

Elena shrugged. "Honestly, I'm passable, but I'm

much better with landscapes. And I suck at Photoshop. My mom rocks it, though."

Jenna's attention shifted to Tyree. "She's here, right? Why don't you ask her?"

"You should," Elena said. "Ask her tomorrow."

"I thought you and I were going to Fredericksburg tomorrow." She'd told him that she wanted to see the Hill Country, and since Eli was at Jeremy's for the next few days, and since Tyree needed to talk to some local vintners about carrying their labels at The Fix, he'd agreed, looking forward to the chance to get to know his daughter better.

"Right," she said, toying with the stem of her glass. "I meant in the evening." She put the glass down, then rubbed her brow. "After we get back."

He frowned, but assumed her odd behavior was because she knew as well as he did that Eva would turn him down flat. "I'll ask," he said, then turned to Jenna. "But don't hold your breath."

Chapter Ten

EVA SAW THE LONG, black limousine the moment she stepped through the ornate doors of the Driskill's main entrance. Of course she didn't think a thing of it; after all, Austin boasted both a moneyed population and a steady stream of celebrities. It was only when the driver got out and opened the back door for Elena that Eva did a double take.

Her daughter was decked out in a pale blue wrap-around skirt, a form-fitting tank top, and over-sized sunglasses. She looked like she belonged in a limo, and when she waved at Eva, her grin lit up the morning.

"Awesome, isn't it? Aunt Marianne booked it for the entire day. And there's wine back here. Liquor, too."

"I guess we don't need to go to Fredericksburg. We

can just drive around town and drink the limo's stash."

"Don't go into stand-up comedy, Mom."

Eva smirked, then nodded at the driver as she followed Elena into the limousine. It was fully loaded, with a television, DVD player, privacy screen, sunroof, and a control panel suggesting even more features Eva couldn't imagine. Possibly a hot tub. Or a rocket launcher.

"This is incredible," she said, as the driver pulled away from the hotel. "Marianne really set this up?"

"Yeah, cool, isn't it?"

"I think I'm paying her entirely too much."

"Ha ha. Don't you even think about the cost. This is a day to enjoy."

Eva nodded and pulled out her phone. "I'm not arguing. I did a little research last night. If we take RM 1431, that takes us through someplace called Lago Vista and then onto Marble Falls, and both are supposed to be pretty. Then we go up to Johnson City and over to Fredericksburg. And there are wineries along the way that we can stop in at. See?" She held up her phone and pointed to the map.

"And then when we're in Fredericksburg, there are some darling places to shop and ton of wineries around the town. And as for food, we can do traditional German or find something else. Apparently, they have everything. Even the Nimitz Museum, which is the National Museum of the Pacific War. I'm not sure why it's landlocked in Texas, but we can check it out, and if it's cool, you should mention it to your father. There's probably a lot of Naval stuff he'd be interested in."

"Mmm. Yeah. I'll do that."

Eva shot a glance toward Elena, then decided the unenthusiastic response was because she didn't want her mother dragging her to a museum on a drinking and shopping day. Fair enough.

"There's also a place called Wildseed Farms that looks fun. They sell the flowers, but also crafts and ice cream." She stressed the last word and got a laugh from Elena. But it seemed a little hollow, too.

She sat her phone on the seat between them, crossed her arms, and said, "Okay, what's going on? This was your idea, and I'm the one who's giddy."

"I'm fine," Elena said. "I'm just super tired. I didn't sleep well at all last night." She reached over and grabbed Eva's phone, clicking the side button to darken the display. Then she reached down and dropped it into Eva's purse. "So, the limo's pretty cool, right? And there's music."

As she turned toward the console, Eva grabbed her phone again.

"Mom! It's our time. Don't be hanging on your phone."

"I just want to follow the map. There are places we might want to stop. And—okay. What are we doing on the east side of the highway?"

Elena's brows rose. "I don't know how to get to Fredericksburg and neither do you. Let's trust the driver, okay?"

But as they talked, the limo made a right turn off Airport Boulevard and into a neighborhood. Eva kept her head down, not sure if she should laugh or shout.

In the end, she decided on a maternal scowl as she lifted her head to face her daughter. "So," she said. "Who are we picking up?"

"Ah, um."

"That's what I thought." Definitely a laugh, though she wasn't going to let it show. "Would have been nice if you'd told me you'd invited him. I might have dressed better." She wore linen drawstring pants and light cotton T-shirt.

"You look great."

Eva wanted to disagree—she'd barely put on any make-up—but held her tongue. Elena obviously had orchestrated a chance to spend time with both her parents. It was not—repeat, *not*—a date, and so it didn't matter what Eva looked like.

Not that she could escape, even if she wanted to. Because there he was, coming out of the charming little limestone house nestled in among the oak and pecan trees.

He was wearing jeans that hugged his thighs and a short-sleeved navy blue T-shirt that stretched tight across his well-muscled chest and incredibly broad shoulders. She had a sudden, visceral memory of her fingertips stroking his skin, the light dusting of chest hair rough beneath her touch. Of resting her head on his chest as they lay naked together. Of the hard, safe lines of his body.

Okay, stop. Just stop.

She took a deep breath designed to reset her senses, grabbed a tissue from the box on the back console, and wiped the line of sweat that had formed on her upper lip and at the back of her neck.

If Elena noticed, Eva was blaming it on the early onset of menopause, truth be damned.

After killing the engine, the driver came around and opened the curbside door, and Elena scrambled out, her squeal of, "Check it out! We're going in style," making Tyree laugh, the low rumbling baritone doing all sorts of pleasant things to Eva's body.

Pleasant, and yet inconvenient.

There was no denying that her attraction to the man hadn't faded over the years. If anything, it had intensified. He was a man now, not a boy. He owned a business. He knew how to roll with the punches. And from what little she'd seen with him and Elena, he was a pretty damn amazing father.

What he wasn't, was hers. And she needed to remember that. She wasn't going to have a fling with the man she'd once had a fling with. Especially since that fling had shifted both their lives off course. True, that had been her father's fault. But they were both more than twenty years down different paths now.

And life was confusing enough without adding fresh layers of lust to the mix.

All of which sounded incredibly rational and intelligent. Too bad for Eva that rational thought and intelligence seemed to go flying off into the hinterlands whenever Tyree so much as looked at her.

Still, she'd closed the door Wednesday night. So she knew she *could* be strong. She just had to remember to actually do it.

But surely today wouldn't be much of a problem. After all, they could hardly get wild and naked in a limo with their daughter sitting between them.

She started to slide toward the door, intending to get out and say hello properly, but then he was stooping down to climb inside, and he stopped midway in, his eyes fixed on her, his face a mixture of surprise and pleasure.

She couldn't help it; she burst into laughter. "You, too?"

A charming grin lit his face. "Do you remember that Disney movie they remade with Lindsay Lohan?"

"*The Parent Trap?*" She glanced past him to where Elena stood just outside the limo. "One of Elena's favorite films growing up."

He slid all the way into the limo and settled on the long bench seat perpendicular to hers, so close that their knees brushed. She shifted sideways, because even that tiny bit of contact was setting off sparks of awareness that were far too disturbing and very confusing.

"I'm not at all surprised," Tyree said.

"*What?*" Her head flew up to meet his eyes.

"About the movie. What did you think I—"

"Never mind."

"This is going to be fabulous," Elena said, climbing into the car and rescuing Eva from her own idiocy.

Then the driver shut the door, and a few moments later they were underway.

"Okay," Elena said. "Who's drinking what? And no fair saying nothing because we have a limo, and sober is not the point of this trip."

Tyree and Eva exchanged smiles. "You raised a bossy little thing."

"It's a trait she inherited from her father."

"Yeah, yeah," Elena chirped. "You're both comedians. Come on. I want drink orders."

"Whiskey," Eva said, then saw Tyree smile. "What?"

"Not a thing. I'll have the same."

"Gotcha covered," Elena said, then knelt in front of the bar as she poured their drinks, then poured a glass of wine for herself.

They chatted about their itinerary for a bit, with both Elena and Eva breathing a surreptitious sigh of relief when Tyree told them that the Nimitz Museum was fabulous, but that he'd been there several times.

"Are we going that 1431 route?" Eva said. "Because it looks like there's a winery right before we get to Marble Falls."

"I'm not sure what he's doing," Tyree said, bending to look out the window. "Unless he knows about a wreck that's not showing on your map, I would have thought he'd be on the highway by now. Not over here in Crestview where—"

"What?" Eva said, looking up from her phone to find Tyree giving the stinkeye to their daughter. "Oh, dear."

"Why are we in the Crestview neighborhood, Elena?"

"What's in Crestview?" Eva asked.

"Some darling little houses. Including Brent's." At her blank look, he continued, "The man who showed you back to my office. One of my partners at The Fix."

"And a single dad," Elena hurried to say. "He asked if I could babysit today. And Marianne had already booked the limo, and I was afraid if I told you guys then one of you would bail, and honestly, don't you want to catch up? If nothing else, Tyree needs to hear about every single adorable thing I did growing up. And, honestly, I was pretty adorable. That's bound to take all day."

She paused for a breath, and Eva tried very hard not to laugh. Based on Tyree's expression, he was trying as well.

"You know," Tyree said, "I would have been happy to simply take your mother out tonight—even tonight and tomorrow if that's what it took to convey your awesomeness," he added, with a hint of mischief in his eyes. "No wild scheme necessary."

"Yeah, but I wanted to make sure you guys talked now. And, you know, had a nice time. I mean, since she's leaving tomorrow."

Tyree turned from Elena to Eva. "You're leaving?"

She thought she heard disappointment in his voice, but she pushed it away. She'd decided to leave. She needed to leave. It was best if she left. "I don't live here, remember? And I have a business back home, and I'm heading to Vancouver on Sunday. A very long-awaited vacation."

She turned toward Elena with her best stern-mom expression. "I'd intended to leave today, but my daughter convinced me to spend the extra time with her."

Elena waved the words away. "You've spent time with me for twenty-three years. Honestly, you must be sick to death of me. But guess who you haven't seen for twenty-three years…" She trailed off with a significant look at Tyree who, being a ham, spread his arms at his sides and flashed a crazy grin.

"You're really okay with this?" she asked him.

"With spending time with the one person who can

tell me what my daughter's first word was? Yeah. I'm okay with that."

"All right, then. And it was *no*. Go figure."

They pulled up in front of a charming wood and stone house, and the driver started around to Elena's door.

"One thing," Tyree said. "I thought you said I should talk to your mom about doing the—"

"Pictures?" Elena cut in. "Yeah, you're right. I don't know what I was thinking. Hard to do that if she leaves."

Tyree's brow furrowed, but he didn't say anything else. So Eva asked. "What pictures?"

"No big deal," Elena assured her. "Go on. Have fun." She leaned over and kissed Eva, then gave Tyree's cheek a kiss, too. "Have fun, you two. Have as much fun as you want to."

Then she hopped out of the car and hurried up the sidewalk where the man Eva had met on Wednesday was opening the door and waving at the limo. Eva caught a glimpse of a dark-haired little cutie before the door shut, and her daughter disappeared, and she was left alone in the back of a limo with a man she was wildly attracted to … but who was also absolutely, one-hundred percent off-limits for at least a dozen reasons.

None of which she could actually call to mind at the moment.

Chapter Eleven

THEY WERE ALREADY tipsy by the time they reached Fredericksburg, and not because of the whiskey in the limo—well, not entirely. No, they'd stopped at three vineyards along the way, enjoyed the tastings and the cheese plates, and Tyree had even taken the card of one of the vintners, promising to call him on Monday to discuss using his red blend as the featured local wine at The Fix.

"There's a winery right on Main Street," Tyree told her. "Want me to have the driver stop there?"

"No way," she said, the shaking motion of her head feeling far too exaggerated. "But I do need food. And I think we should go to a German restaurant. That's what the town's mostly known for, right?"

"Used to be. I think a lot of fine dining and locally-sourced restaurants have moved in. But if you want German, we'll have German." He checked his watch. "We'll hit Der Lindenbaum. Touristy, but good. And then I know just the place for dessert."

She grinned. "I didn't realize I had a tour guide."

"Your wish, my command," he said, apparently relishing the idea of taking care of her. Honestly, she didn't mind. She used to be able to drink like a fish, but she'd cut out alcohol entirely when she was pregnant and breastfeeding, and then David only drank wine. She still had the occasional drink, but she'd pretty much consumed a year's supply just in the drive to this adorable little town.

Tyree, who probably remembered the days when she could out drink a football team, was watching her with amusement.

"What?"

"You're adorable when you're wasted."

"Oh, no. This is not about me being adorable. The only adorable we're allowed to talk about is Elena. And believe me, she qualifies."

"All right, then. Tell me another."

She'd already told him the story of Elena's birth, which had been ridiculously easy for her, but hard on David, who'd passed out from the sight of blood. She might have been imagining it, but she thought she'd seen a smug glint in Tyree's eyes when she told him that. After all, as a combat veteran, surely he'd had no trouble with his own son's birth.

She wished she'd been able to see him with Elena. At only six pounds at birth, she'd been healthy but tiny, and Eva could imagine Tyree holding her in the palm of his big hand. Or patting her tiny back as he held her against his broad shoulder after a feeding.

Blinking, she turned away, suddenly acutely aware of all they'd missed.

"You okay?"

"Sure." She gathered herself and turned back. "Just feeling the alcohol."

"We'll get food in you soon." He reached for the intercom, then told the driver to pull over when he could. A short time later, the limo drew to a stop on a side street and the driver let them out. Tyree told him to do whatever he wanted for the next few hours; that they were going to eat and explore, and he'd text when they were ready to get back in the limo.

"Nice way to travel," she said as they walked toward the restaurant. "I still can't believe Marianne did this."

"Are you sure she did?"

Eva shot him a sideways glance. "Do you know something I don't, or do you just think kids are inherently sneaky?"

"There's some definite sneakiness potential," he said. "Knowing Elena a bit now, I think she got more than her share of the gene."

"Hmm."

They walked past shops and restaurants until finally Tyree paused, then pulled open a door to reveal a homey restaurant that smelled amazing. She stepped in and sighed with pleasure. "I'm pretty much going to gorge myself on wurst. Be prepared."

He laughed, but she wasn't joking. And after she'd ordered, she pulled out her phone and opened her credit card app. Then she burst out laughing.

"What?"

"You, sir, are a fine judge of character. An authorization for a limo charge." She rolled her eyes. "I told her she could stay on my credit card until she's out of grad school, but starting this year, she has to get a job to cover her charges."

"She knew you'd figure it out," he said. "If nothing else, your friend would have been clueless when you thanked her." He reached across the table and took her hand, the connection sending a flurry of sparks skittering along her skin. "I guess the real question is whether you're going to thank our daughter."

She looked down at their joined hands, drew in a breath, then lifted her eyes to meet his. "Yeah, I definitely am."

"Good," he said. "Me, too."

She was relieved when the waitress arrived with their food. There was too much emotion—and way too many cravings—swirling around inside of her. And mixed with the alcohol that was a bad combination.

She considered the food a temporary reset button, and dug in, eating more than she should to soak up some of the wine and whiskey. They talked while they ate, and she asked if his son was as sneaky as his daughter. "Not yet," Tyree said. "But he's only sixteen. Give him time."

On the whole, though, they didn't talk about Eli or Teiko. Just enough for Tyree to give the basic overview to catch her up with his life. The point of this day, after all, was for the two of them to reconnect— to reconnect *as parents*—and to talk about Elena.

And, yeah, to eat and drink and shop.

They continued on with that part of the itinerary after they'd devoured some truly delicious wurst. "Dessert?" Tyree asked as soon as they were back on the street.

"What are you? A bottomless pit? Let's window shop a bit."

They did, strolling along Main Street and looking in the windows of the charming shops. Once or twice they popped in, and in one adorable store, Eva found the perfect T-shirt for Elena. *I'm only bossy because I was born that way.* She reached over and grabbed Tyree's hand, tugging him over to take a look, too.

At first, she didn't even realize they were touching. Then she felt his warmth and the slow burn of awareness curling through her to pool in her lower belly before settling even lower, making her aware of places that had been sadly ignored for some very, very long months.

Casually, she started to tug her hand away, because it felt a little too nice and way too confusing to stay like that. But he tightened his grip, and she was left with the choice of either yanking her hand free or staying connected.

Swallowing, she looked up, only to find him smiling down at her, obviously understanding her dilemma perfectly.

Well, fine.

She kept her hand where it was, feeling smug. Like she'd won that round.

But then he lifted their joint hands and lightly brushed a kiss over the base of her thumb, as if that was the most normal thing to do. As if the sensation didn't send her entire being, body and soul, into a tailspin.

"It really is the perfect shirt for her," he said casually, apparently clueless that her body had gone on high alert. "Should we get it?"

She nodded, because speaking was out of the question. He grabbed the shirt, then led her to the register where he managed to pay with one hand— proving to her that he was deliberately messing with her. But she was okay with that. Because now that she'd gotten over the shock, she had to admit that being messed with felt pretty nice.

So nice, in fact, that when they finally had their fill of shopping and ended up at the Clear River Ice Cream & Bakery shop, she was actually disappointed. Because there was no way to eat a cup of ice cream with a spoon and not use both hands. Not and do it gracefully, anyway.

"We need to get back soon," he said. "It's almost eight."

"I know. I've had a really nice day."

He said nothing for a moment, just looked in her eyes. Then he nodded and held out a spoon of his Chocolate Hazelnut ice cream for her to try. She did, her mouth closing over the spoon as her eyes held his, and though she really wasn't trying to flirt, there was something so damn sensual about the moment that she had to fight the urge to squirm in her chair just to release some of the sexual tension that was flooding through her, as delicious and sweet as warm chocolate sauce.

"I'll call the driver," he said, his voice tight.

She nodded. "That's a good idea."

At least, she thought it was a good idea until they climbed into the car. The sun was still up, but it was setting fast, and with the darkened windows, the car's interior had a sultry, sensual feel. Or maybe that was just Eva.

Either way, she sat on the back seat feeling hyper-aware of everything—especially the man sitting beside her.

"You don't mind, do you? I rode sideways going in, but I think I've had enough to drink to make that unpleasant going back."

"Of course I don't mind," she said. Then said

nothing else for at least fifteen miles because she didn't know what to say. So she just listened as he talked about the food and the leather goods store where he'd bought a wallet and the cute shirt they'd picked up for Elena.

"I'm babbling, aren't I?"

"What?" she said. "Oh, no."

"Then why aren't you saying anything?"

"Oh. I. Well. This is going to sound odd, but I think I'm a little nervous." She turned sideways enough to see his face, relieved to have confessed that much of it.

"Really? That's funny."

"Excuse me?"

"I just mean that's why *I'm* babbling."

"Oh." She frowned. "You mean you're nervous, too."

"Pretty much."

"What have you got to be nervous about?" She heard the breathiness in her voice and wondered if he did, too.

"Probably the same thing you do." That time, it was a tease she heard.

"Oh. Right." She nodded, her head bobbing foolishly as she tried to drum up some courage. Finally, she turned to him and blurted, "There's something I've been wanting to do."

"Yeah? What—"

But she didn't let him finish the question. Instead,

she leaned into him, which was more awkward than she expected since they were sitting side by side, and she was still tipsy. She bumped his nose, gasped, then found her mouth pressed hard against his, exactly where she'd been aiming in the first place.

He opened to her, his mouth firm and demanding with just a hint of chocolate. And when his hand cupped her head and pulled her closer, she moaned and melted into the kiss. Their mouths locked into a battle, a war, a wild match that she was determined to win, knowing that no matter what, she'd come away satisfied.

Memory flooded over her. The taste of him. The scent. The feel of his fingers on her body, of his tongue teasing her breasts. Beneath her bra, her nipples peaked, and some small part of her brain shouted that this was too much, that she'd regret it in the morning, that she really needed to never drink again.

She told the voice to go to hell and shifted on the seat. And then, because she was feeling far too bold and way too foolish, she moved onto his lap and straddled him.

"*Eva.*" His voice was a low groan, swallowed by an even deeper kiss. She shifted her weight, then gasped as she realized how close they were and how hard he was. She could feel his erection through his jeans, and though she knew she was being completely wanton, she didn't care. She ground against him, wanting even more, but knowing that she would have to stop. That they couldn't take this much further.

But oh, it felt good to just go this far.

His hands stroked her body, the one at her neck sliding down as another crept under her shirt, teasing it up until, finally, his palm closed over her breast and she moaned against his mouth.

He tasted so good. Felt so good. Like the past and the future all rolled into one.

Except he couldn't be…

Her future wasn't here, it was at home, in California. She had a life, and he had a life, and if they kept this up—if she let this lead all the way to sex in a limousine—they'd both regret it in the morning.

Which was a damn shame, really, because at the moment she couldn't think of anything she wanted more than to strip naked and ride him all the way back to Austin.

No.

She broke the kiss, breathing hard as she leaned back, telling herself she was doing the right thing because they were grownups and they needed to pretend like they knew how to play the part.

"I'm sorry," she whispered. "I shouldn't have been so bold. And I definitely started that." She climbed off him, then scrambled to the long seat where he'd spent the ride up.

"It's okay," he said. He sounded breathless, maybe

even a little frustrated, but thankfully not angry. "I like bold women."

She sighed, relieved that he was being so sweet. Another man might be angry that she'd put on the brakes. "It's just that I wanted—"

She cut herself off, feeling ridiculous.

"What?" he asked.

She drew in a breath, then let it out slowly. Then she met his eyes and shrugged. "I wanted to see if it was like I remembered."

The corner of his mouth twitched. "And was it?"

"No," she said honestly. "It was better."

"WELL, THIS IS MY STOP." Eva paused in front of her hotel room door, then gently tugged her hand free, and Tyree immediately mourned the loss of her warm touch. "Thanks for walking me in. You didn't have to."

"Sure I did. Had to make sure you got home safe, right?"

"I—" She swallowed, then took a deep breath, obviously trying to decide how to say whatever she had to say.

Honestly, he didn't want to hear it.

"It's just that—"

"Eva?"

"Yes?"

"Hush."

Her mouth opened in surprise, and he leaned in, taking full advantage of the moment, relieved when she didn't immediately pull away, but kissed him back, long and slow, until she finally cupped her palm against his cheek and drew back slowly, her eyes on his.

"You know we can't," she whispered.

"Actually, I don't know that at all."

She shot him a frown. "I'm leaving in about twelve hours. I don't want—"

"What?"

He watched her face as she ordered her thoughts, and he knew from the shadow in her eyes that he wasn't going to win this argument.

Finally, she drew in a breath. "I have a lot of good memories of being with you. And a few new ones from today as well. I don't want to tarnish them with goodbye sex. Especially when…" She trailed off with a shrug. "Never mind."

"Tell me."

He watched as she debated, then saw her concede defeat. "I'm not exactly nineteen anymore."

"Aren't you?" He took a step back, his eyes looking her up and down, and his fingers following suit, tracing the curve of her ribcage down to her waist and then over those curvy hips that had felt so good straddling him. "No," he whispered. "I guess you're not."

"Tyree." His name sounded like a plea, but he wasn't certain what she was begging for. "I'm sorry," she said, shattering his hopes. "We share a daughter, Tiger. We can't let it get awkward."

"Tiger," she repeated, and his heart actually skipped a beat.

She looked as surprised as he did. "It just slipped out."

It was the name she'd only called him in bed. A secret endearment, just between the two of them. And it told him one hell of a lot about where her head was.

He wanted to press her, and in light of that slip, he was certain he'd win. He wanted her comfort. Wanted to lose himself inside her.

But she'd said no, and he wanted to honor her, too.

Still, would it be so bad to just have a taste…?

He forced the thought away. Better to work together like adults. To get to know each other, even long distance, so they could quit dancing around the lust and settle in as friends. As Elena's parents.

His cock didn't like that idea as much, but all things considered, Tyree wasn't inclined to give his cock much say in the discussion.

She was right after all. She was leaving tomorrow.

Unless, of course, he could figure out a way to change her mind.

Chapter Twelve

SHE OVERSLEPT, naturally, and now Eva hurried to toss all of her crap into her duffel bag so she could race down to the taxi stand and get to the airport in time to catch her plane.

It was Saturday, and Elena had emailed sometime during the night to say that she'd been invited by someone at the University to go to a picnic sponsored by the Community and Regional Planning program where she intended to apply after her gap year. She'd said she hated missing seeing Eva off, but that she'd fly home to San Diego soon, maybe for the fourth of July holiday.

Not that Eva begrudged her daughter the picnic, but if she'd only picked up the phone that morning, then Eva might not be rushing now. And what if the bellman had to call for a taxi? *Dammit.*

In the hall, she pressed the button to call the

elevator, silently cursing as it crept to her floor at its own lethargic pace. Finally, she made it on and down to the lobby. Then she raced out the door, waved for the bellman to signal a taxi, and then froze on the sidewalk as she saw Tyree standing across the street, his large frame leaning casually against the side of a slate gray Jeep Grand Cherokee.

"Need a lift?" he asked, jaywalking toward her.

"Depends. Does that thing fly? I'm ridiculously late." She waited for him to make some reference to last night, but he seemed to be all business. And since that attitude made it much easier to walk away, she decided that she was grateful.

He hoisted her duffel, then held out his free hand. "What time's your flight?"

She told him, and he looked at his watch, then let out a low whistle. "If I was smart, I'd tell you there was no way, just to keep you here a few more hours."

"Yeah, but we both know you're not that bright."

His laughter rolled over her like a sweet caress. "True that. Come on. I'll get you there on time. Getting through security quickly's on you, though."

"I'll take that deal." Gratefully, she hurried to match his stride as he crossed illegally once more.

Once inside the car, she relaxed into the leather seats. "Thank you. This is much better than a taxi. And, frankly, better than Elena's tiny Honda."

"Speaking of Elena," he said as he pulled into

traffic, "I wanted to talk to you about her. Parent to parent, I mean."

"Sure. Actually, wait." She shifted in the seat to look at him. "I never told you what time my plane left. How did you know when to linger outside the hotel?"

"I'll give you one guess."

She flopped back in her seat. "Our little conniver. Does she even have an event at the University?"

"Actually, I think she does. Tonight."

"Well, at least it was only ninety-five percent untrue. Wouldn't want her to lie to her mother."

He grinned.

"What?"

"You two. You work well together. And it's easy to see how much you love each other."

The words warmed her. "Yeah? Thanks."

"That's sort of what I wanted to talk to you about. See? I did have a reason for wanting to drive you. A reason other than just seeing you again, I mean."

"Oh." She licked her suddenly dry lips. "Why?"

"It occurred to me that Elena's never had two parents. I mean, that she remembers."

"Um, okay?"

"And Eli's never met either of you."

A sad smile touched her lips. "And I would love to meet him. I'm sure I'll come back. I'll try to come for a week before the end of the summer."

"That's one idea. I'm thinking along different lines."

"Oh. Okay. What?"

"Well, it seems to me that you and I have had some big responsibilities dropped into our laps."

"We have?"

"Sure. I mean, there are life things we need to be considering. We're a family now, Eva. Have you thought about that?"

She swallowed, realizing he was right. And she most definitely hadn't thought about it. Not the way he meant. As if they were a unit.

"Families have obligations," he said. "Sometimes awesome ones. Sometimes inconvenient ones."

Something in his tone caught her attention, and she crossed her arms tight across her chest. "Are you saying I'm running away?"

He took his eyes off the road long enough to look at her directly for one beat. "Well, aren't you?"

Her temper flared. "Now, hold on. I'm going on vacation. I've been planning it for ages. And in case you missed the memo, our daughter is an adult."

The anger, of course, was for herself. Because he was right. Elena *was* an adult. But she was a young adult, still in school, who'd just learned that her supposedly dead father was alive and that she also had a half-brother whom she had yet to meet.

And Eva was traipsing off to Vancouver?

Yeah, she really was running away. Why the hell hadn't she seen it?

"It's hard to figure out your own head sometimes," he said, after she told him all that. "Sometimes you have to look at it from someone else's perspective."

"Like yours?"

"Happy to provide you perspective anytime you want," he said with a seductive little grin.

She sighed and flopped back in her seat. "You realize what the biggest problem here is, don't you?"

"What's that?"

"You. You're what I was running away from."

He reached over and squeezed her hand. "Oh, I wouldn't let that bother you. That's a problem I can live with."

EVA CALLED the airline from the car to cancel her ticket, banking the credit for when she finally did return to California. Then she called Marianne and explained the situation and asked her to cancel the Vancouver flight and the hotel.

"I hope this is because you're getting laid," Marianne said. "Because I really miss you. But it's worth it if you're getting good sex."

"You have no idea how lucky you are that I don't have you on speaker right now," Eva said, making her friend laugh like a loon.

She shook her head, then told Marianne she'd see her in two weeks. After that, she'd have to get back, as she had some wedding shoots and a Sweet Sixteen party on the books.

"There, wasn't that easy?" Tyree asked.

"For you. You're not rearranging your life. And it just occurred to me that I'm now homeless. I gave up my room at the Driskill."

"I'm sure they'd be happy to book you another. But I do have an alternate solution."

"I am *not* staying at your house. So just forget it."

"As tempting as you are, that wasn't the solution."

"Oh." It was, she knew, stupid to be disappointed. "What, then?"

"Elena said to tell you that the apartment she's watching is a two bedroom."

"Look at you two. Quite the schemers."

He shook his head. "I had nothing to do with living arrangements. I just have a vested interest in keeping you here."

"Yeah? Why?" She was playing with fire, but she couldn't help herself. Despite having her plans completely explode, she was having an exceptionally good day.

"Why? Because I want you here."

"Oh." She felt the tug of her smile. "Well, that's a reason."

He reached over and squeezed her hand quickly. Then, when he started to pull it back, she held on. She saw him glance down, and she just shrugged. For a second, she thought he'd pull away. But then he relaxed, and they rode in silence the rest of the way to The Fix.

"Why are we here?" she asked as he pulled into the single space in the alley. "I assumed you'd be taking me to Elena's."

"Just one quick stop here, if that's okay. We've got a staff meeting this morning, and since Elena's on staff now, I thought I'd introduce you around."

"Uh-huh. In other words, you and our daughter have some other scheme in your pocket and this is where you spring it on me?"

"Also a valid possibility," he said, looking so contrite that she actually giggled. "Fine. I admit I'm curious." She waited until he'd killed the engine, then climbed out of the car. He opened the thick metal back door and led her into the bar. As soon as they reached the main rooms, she paused to soak it all in.

This was, she realized, the first time she'd had a good look around. Her first time here, she'd been too nervous to see anything going in, and too pissed to pay attention to anything going out.

Now, she had to admit she liked what she saw. It was fun, but cozy. A traditional bar, but different. It looked like the kind of place where regulars gathered. It looked like a place that felt like home.

"It's great," she said. "You really did it. Your own place. Food. Drink. Just like you always said you wanted."

She saw the pride in his eyes as he nodded. "I love

this place. It's been damn good to me. And I'm doing everything I can to not lose it."

"Elena told me some of that," she admitted.

"And now we're hoping to tell you a little more. Come on."

They moved to a front alcove by the window where a small group, including Elena, already sat. She'd met Brent during her earlier visit, but Tyree introduced the other two—who were clearly a couple —as Reece and Jenna.

"It's really great to meet you," Jenna said as she stood up. "And that's not just because we totally want to hit you up for work."

Tyree laughed. "Way to blow the lead, Jenna. I haven't told her yet."

The petite redhead put her hands on her hips and scowled at him, so ferociously that Eva wouldn't lay odds against her. "You were in a car for almost an hour to the airport and back and you didn't think to mention what we wanted to talk about?" She shook her head, clearly exasperated. "Men."

"They only want you for your camera, Mom," Elena said, to which Tyree nodded. "Pretty much. I know that's all I want."

She bit back a laugh, then collapsed into a chair. "Okay, slow down. What's the deal?"

The deal, apparently, was that they needed images of the first five winners—the fifth contest was coming up fast—of the Man of the Month calendar contest to use in the actual calendar. "And promo shots for general advertising," Jenna said. "And then we'll need six through twelve, too, but if you can get the first set done that would be a huge load off. Plus we're doing a cookbook, so we're hoping to get some staged food shots, too."

"Don't forget Megan's idea," Reece said.

"Oh, right." Jenna turned back to Eva. "Megan's started working with me doing marketing, and she had this great idea that we'd start putting together postcards and flyers and social media posts of all the guys who are actually entered. You know, promoting the contest before it takes place. We're always at capacity, so I honestly didn't think about it, which is lame. But she's so right. It's a huge way to up exposure for the bar overall. But that's twelve shots we need every two weeks. So far, we've always had twelve entrants," she explained.

She looked at the other four. "I think that's it." When nobody corrected her, she turned to Eva. "Yeah, that's it. Any interest? Elena said she could take the pictures, but she also said you were a billion times better. And that you could clean up the images if they need it."

"I'm not sure about the billion, but I definitely have more experience. It's my job. It's her hobby. And as for taking it on, if it will help you out, then why not?"

"That's great," Tyree said, but she interrupted him by raising her hand.

"I just have one tiny condition."

They all looked at each other. "Shoot," Jenna said.

"I want him in the contest." She looked at Tyree with the most innocent smile she could conjure. Then she shifted her attention to Elena. "Don't you think so, sweetheart?"

Elena managed an equally stoic expression, although Eva could see the laughter dancing behind her eyes. "Oh, definitely."

"I mean, if I'm shooting the men who are going to be on the bar's advertising, I think the owner should be among them." She didn't bother asking if the others agreed; she could tell from their expressions they considered it a totally kickass idea.

"So?" she asked Tyree. "I guess it's up to you."

"Then I guess you're staying," he said. "And I guess I'll be strutting my stuff a week from Wednesday."

Chapter Thirteen

TYREE HAD EXPECTED Eva to take the portraits of the men inside The Fix, but that wasn't her plan. "I'll do that, of course. But I want to get to know the guys out in the world first. That'll inform how I want to position them in The Fix."

She told him she intended to shoot them at their work and then at a few locations around the city before scheduling the final shoot for the bar. "Fortunately, all the winners so far are local, so we can take our time."

He couldn't argue with that, though he'd wanted her inside the bar and close by him. Wanted it bad enough, in fact, that he spent some time manipulating the schedule so that he could spend a few hours outside the bar when she did. Ostensibly so that he could represent The Fix if anyone came along from the local paper or a news feed. But the truth was that now that he'd persuaded her to stay a bit longer in Austin, he didn't want her out of his sight.

Initially, he'd told himself that having her stay was for Elena's benefit. But that, of course, was bullshit. *He* wanted her near. *He* wanted her close.

But that desire was a double-edged sword, because every night when he was alone, he felt the shadow. Because if he let Eva in, didn't that mean letting Teiko go?

Those rumblings haunted him in the dark, but they were easy enough to push aside during the day, and so he pushed them shamelessly. Tamped down the demons and joined her as she worked.

They went to KIKX, and Eva took dozens of shots of Nolan in his studio. For Reece, she photographed him doing renovations in his father's kitchen. And when she took Spencer's initial shots, they spent a few hours puttering around the old Drysdale Mansion, a fabulous property that Spencer and Brooke were working on—tailed by their ever-present camera crew—when they weren't jamming on the renovations at The Fix.

On the day she shot Cameron on the UT campus, he and Eva stayed behind after Cameron cut out to go meet Mina. They spent the next few hours chatting about Elena and San Diego and pretty much everything as they navigated the maze of buildings to reach the manicured grounds outside the LBJ Library on the University's eastern edge. Finally, they settled on the hill by the fountain, and Eva pointed her camera at him, even though he'd tossed his hands up as if to ward her off.

"Oh, no," she said. "I want some of you. Besides, you'll win next week. I might as well get ahead of the game."

"I might win," he agreed with a grin. "I mean, I am pretty awesome." He'd been lying on his back watching the sky, but now he rolled onto his side and propped his head up with his hands.

She laughed. "Why are you fishing for compliments?"

"Compliments aren't what I'm fishing for."

She narrowed her eyes suspiciously. "No?"

"I mean, I *am* pretty awesome. But that's just a state of being." He shrugged. "You should compliment me on something I'm willing to work hard at perfecting."

Her expression turned suspicious, but she played along. "And that would be…?"

He crooked a finger. "Come here, and I'll tell you."

He saw the awareness in her eyes as she leaned in. "You know what? I think maybe you should just show me."

He cupped the back of her head. "I think that sounds like a delicious idea," he murmured before tugging her down so that her arm rested on his chest, and her lips covered his.

It was a more intimate position than he'd intended, their balance thrown off by the steepness of the hill, and he was afraid she'd pull away, although, dear Lord, he didn't want her to. Because right then, he thought that her mouth was the sweetest thing he'd ever tasted, and the heat from this kiss combined with the heat of the sun beating down on them made him almost fear that they'd both spontaneously combust at any moment.

But what a way to go.

Far too soon, she broke the kiss, then rose just enough so she could meet his eyes. "I've been wanting to do that again since the moment I decided to stay."

"Thank goodness," he said, then waggled his brows. "Wanna go back to my place?"

She laughed. "Yes. But no." She shifted so that she was sitting on him, straddling his waist. "I'm still not sure this is a good idea," she said softly, her words making him feel cold. Both because he didn't want to hear them, and because he actually agreed with them. "But I want this too much to stop completely."

"Completely?"

"I mean I want to take it slow. Is that okay?"

He reached up and cupped her cheek, then looked deep into those dark, beautiful eyes. "Sugar, that sounds just about perfect."

Her smile seemed to light her from the inside, and she shifted her face so that she could kiss the palm of his hand. The sensation was unexpectedly erotic, and he felt the pull of her lips all the way down to his cock. Christ, he wanted her. But she was right. Slow was better.

"Eva," he murmured. "About that slow thing."

"Yeah?"

"Kiss me," he demanded. "Kiss me long and slow."

Her lips twitched with amusement, and then she bent over, brushed her lips over his, and did exactly what he asked.

ANY LINGERING FEARS that Eli or Elena would find the new family arrangement to be awkward or weird or untenable were quashed the first time that Elena and Eva came to Tyree's place for a family dinner.

It was, he thought, the perfect mixture of chaos and fun.

Elena had brought some Nintendo gadget that made Eli's eyes bug out, and he swore that he'd been intending to ask for one for his birthday. When she'd plugged the small device into the television, basically turning it into a gaming console, Tyree's usually calm and collected teenager went absolutely apeshit.

"She picked the perfect ice breaker," Tyree commented as he returned to the kitchen after taking a peek at the newly acquainted brother and sister hunched over their controllers as they killed bad guys —or possibly aliens—on the television screen.

"It wasn't as altruistic as you think," Eva said from where she was perched on a barstool watching Tyree finish putting together the enchiladas he was making for dinner. "Eva's been a gaming fanatic since she was fifteen. That gizmo was her Christmas present last December. She begged me not to get her any little presents and to put all the money I'd budgeted for her toward it. So I'm going to go out on a limb and say that she and Eli are going to get along even better than we'd hoped."

"I think you may be right," he said, then tossed aside the oven mitt he'd used to pull out the dish and move it onto a trivet.

He came around the bar and sat on the stool beside her, the words she just spoke echoing in his head. "The budget," he repeated, feeling like a complete ass. "Hell, Eva, I never thought to ask. Is being here messing you up financially?"

He'd assumed she had money. Because, frankly, when he'd known her in San Diego she'd had lots of it. Or, at least, her father had.

She shook her head. "No, I told you. I was going on vacation. So, actually, you saved me a ton on the hotel I'm not staying at." She flashed a grin as if to reassure him she wasn't upset about missing her trip. "And don't forget, Jenna's paying me the same as the photographer who trotted off to Milan."

"Still, I'm sorry. I just assumed you could afford it."

She pressed her hand over his. "It's fine. But, yeah, my dad cut me off. No more resources from him from the day I filed for divorce from David. And everything in his estate went to charity, with the exception of some boxes of family memorabilia."

Tyree cringed, despising the man even more than he already did.

"That's where I found the letter from him confessing that he'd only pretended you were dead. And the letter wasn't even to me. I guess he just wanted to clear his conscience. And there were five letters from you to me. I'd never seen even one of them before."

A hard ball of anger settled in his stomach, and, frankly, it was a good thing the old man was dead. Because if he wasn't, Tyree would have been tempted to hop on a plane to San Diego and go have a few words.

"He screwed us both over," she said gently, obviously reading his mind. "But all we can do now is go forward." She met his eyes. "Like this," she added, then bent forward and kissed him, slow and sweet and so tender it melted that ball of steel that had formed in his gut, replacing it with a building heat that fired his blood and made him regret that the kids were in the living room.

"Whoa. Nice work, Dad," Eli's voice shattered the moment, and they burst apart like guilty teenagers.

Speaking of the kids…

"Don't mind me," Eli said, holding his hands up. "I just wanted to check on dinner."

"Five minutes," Tyree said.

Eli's brow rose. "Yeah? You work quick, Dad."

He tossed a dishrag at his son. "Twerp," he said, as the boy ran out, and Eva laughed.

"He really is great," she said, and Tyree had to completely agree.

They ended up eating the enchiladas on TV trays in the living room, which wasn't exactly the family meal he'd envisioned. But the kids wanted to finish their game, and then Eva suggested they watch a movie after that. So once the enchiladas had been devoured, the kids reluctantly unplugged the Nintendo and they surfed the streaming services until they found —of all things—the original Disney *Parent Trap*.

Both Tyree and Eva insisted on watching it, even though Elena seemed completely clueless as to why they were both so amused by the idea.

And although both kids had protested at first— especially Eli, who begged for "anything from this millennium"—they'd ended up enjoying it. Which Tyree considered a bonus, especially since the original movie was more than half a century old. Not quite a millennium, but still ancient for a teen.

It had even spawned a conversation about California, though the story was set at the top of the state, and Elena and Eva had come from San Diego.

"It would be totally cool to live there," Eli said. "I mean, I could learn to surf. That would be awesome."

Best of all, Tyree had spent the evening on the couch with Eva curled up beside him, her head on his chest, and his hand resting on her arm.

The whole evening had been nice. Hell, it had been perfect.

Maybe too perfect. Because the truth was, he could get used to this.

More than that, he wanted to.

Chapter Fourteen

THE BIGGEST DOWNSIDE of Eva shooting all the photographs of the winners was that every few days she needed to just hunker down, focus on her computer screen, and work on cleaning up all the images.

And to do that, she really needed to be alone.

She'd tried taking her laptop to The Fix, but the hum of activity had distracted her, and even when she'd moved into Tyree's back office, she'd been unable to concentrate. Already, the staff and regulars had become her friends, and she wanted to be out there with them, not off hiding in a corner.

Finally, she'd given up and told Tyree that on the days she needed to work in Photoshop, she was going to do it in Elena's apartment with her phone turned off.

Today was one of those days, and though she'd

managed to focus for most of the day, by the time evening rolled around, her mind had begun to wander. Because, dammit, she wanted to be with Tyree.

She told herself to stop acting like a lovesick teenager and finish her work, and the effect of that stern talking-to lasted for a good twenty minutes. Then she found her mind wandering again. Scheming. Justifying. Because why not go to the bar? The images would still be on her computer tomorrow. And it wasn't as if she had a firm deadline to edit the shots. She was simply trying to keep ahead of the work. But surely a few hours on a Monday night wouldn't throw her too far off schedule. Would it?

She told herself that it absolutely wouldn't, decided she might as well listen to the little devil on her shoulder, then stood up to go toss on something more presentable than the cut-off pair of Elena's sweatpants she'd pulled on after her shower that morning. And the tank top, while comfortable in the Austin heat, really wasn't appropriate attire, especially since she was wearing it without a bra.

She'd just stood up to go change when she heard the knock at the front door. She hurried that way, expecting it to be the downstairs neighbor, coming to return the screwdriver she'd borrowed that morning.

Instead, she found herself staring at Tyree.

"Oh," she said, then cursed her utter lack of imagination. Why couldn't she have said something clever or sexy? Probably because at the moment she felt ratty, not sexy, but she stood back and let him enter, anyway.

But as soon as she'd shut the door behind him, she had to rethink that whole sexy thing, because he was looking at her with so much lust that all of her fears about no longer being attractive to him went right out the window. The outfit she wore left very little to the imagination, and if the way his heated gaze was roaming over her—making her blood fire in response —Tyree was more than happy with the way she filled out the shorts and tank.

"Good Lord, woman. You're going to give a man a heart attack."

"I think that's one of the best compliments anyone's ever given me."

"I came over because I wanted to see you. To talk to you. But now…"

He took a step closer.

"What?" Her voice sounded breathless.

"I think I'm going to just skip the talking part," he said, and before she even managed to follow the line of conversation, he had her caged in his arms. His kiss was hot. Deliciously wild. And there was something exciting about being trapped like that in his arms. In knowing that he could do anything he wanted to her in that moment. In hoping that he'd do just that.

As if she'd voiced her fantasy, he took her arms

and thrust them above her head. His palm was big enough that when he crossed her wrists, he was able to hold her there with just one hand. With the other, he pushed up her tank top, making her gasp when he lifted it above her breasts, exposing her nipples.

He bent, taking one in his mouth, then sucking hard before grazing the tender flesh with his teeth. When he pulled his mouth away, he blew a thin stream of air, and she felt her areola tighten in response to the decadent, wonderful sensation.

"You have such beautiful breasts," he murmured, closing his mouth over her again and then slowly kissing his way up, playing his lips along her collarbone with such slow and intimate detail she could feel the pull of his touch all the way down between her thighs. She was throbbing there. Her core clenching with desire, wanting him to fill her. Wanting to feel him inside her.

And at the same time, she didn't want to move. Wanted to stay like this forever, at his mercy, as he teased and tormented her with his mouth and his hands.

"God, Eva," he groaned. "What have you done to me."

She laughed. "I don't know. But I'm really glad you came over."

"I wanted to see you. Hell, I had to see you." He stroked her bottom lip with the pad of his thumb. "Sometimes I think I shouldn't want you this much."

The words were soft but heartfelt.

"The distance," she said. "I know. I have a business in San Diego. You have a business here."

He nodded. "That's part of it. It feels untenable."

"Maybe it doesn't have to be." She hadn't meant to speak the words, but now that she had, she knew they were true. She craved him. Wanted him. And foolish or not, she believed they'd get over these barriers together.

She didn't understand the shadow she saw in his eyes. And with a sudden flash of worry, she realized that he'd said their geographical incompatibility was only part of their problem. "Tyree?"

"Hush," he said. "Let me kiss you." The shadow was gone now, and she wondered if it had only been her imagination. It hadn't been, though. Some part of her knew that. But at the moment, that part of her didn't much care.

"Just kiss me?" Her body felt hyperaware, and her breath caught in her throat. "What if I want more?"

"Oh, baby," he said, his voice thick with longing. And then he did kiss her. A long, hot kiss that felt like a promise. The kind of kiss that led places. And, in this case, it led right into the bedroom when he took her hand and drew her there with him.

"Okay?"

"Oh, yes," she said, then gasped when he moved closer and slowly, deliciously slowly, drew the tank over her head. He tossed it aside, then bent to take

141

her breast fully in his mouth even as his hand slid down her belly and beneath the loose waistband of the cut-off sweats.

She wasn't wearing underwear, and his fingers teased over her trimmed pubic hair before brushing over her clit and making her squeak with pleasure, her legs going so weak she wasn't sure if she could stay upright.

"Please," she murmured, not entirely sure what she was asking for. It didn't matter. He had her well in hand, and after tugging the shorts down, he urged her to sit on the edge of the bed.

"Lie back," he ordered, and she obeyed willingly, biting her lower lip when he pulled the shorts all the way off of her feet, then spread her legs wide, exposing her fully to him.

"Tyree," she said, shifting a little, both aroused and shy. The shyness faded, however when she felt his lips brush her inner thigh as the pad of one thumb teased the back of her knee. It was as if she was a sensual instrument, and he was playing her to perfection. He moved slowly, his mouth and tongue tasting and exploring but never reaching her core.

His fingers danced lightly on her other thigh, moving higher and higher until she arched up in surprise when his fingertip flicked lightly over her clit. "Please," she said, as his lips moved higher, the brush of his close-trimmed beard rubbing her inner thighs in a way that was making her seriously delirious.

And then—oh, dear God—he closed his mouth over her, his tongue teasing her clit as his fingers slid into her. And she was wet—so incredibly wet—and the feel of him was almost more than she could handle. And yet at the same time she wanted more, and she shamelessly bucked her hips, squirming a bit as his mouth worked serious magic on her, taking her higher and higher until before she knew it a firestorm of electricity was crackling through her body, radiating out through her fingers and toes.

It had been so long, so damn long, and she couldn't remember ever coming this hard. Her body shook and she cried out. And the cliche was true because— oh, yes—she actually saw stars.

When her body quit shaking, she realized that he'd maneuvered her all the way onto the bed, and his body was straddling her, his huge erection brushing her lower belly, and making her crave even more. She wanted to feel him inside her. She wanted the connection, the power, the submission of being claimed by this man who had been a part of her for decades, even when they'd been separated by miles and years.

"Kiss me," she demanded, then tasted her own arousal on his lips when he complied. She clutched his back pulling him closer. Her nails scraping, her teeth nibbling. She wanted to be taken and she begged him to thrust inside her. "Please. I'm on birth control and I'm clean. Oh, God, please."

She closed his eyes, arching up as she spread her

legs, felt the weight of him on her, heard his moan of passion as his cock teased her entrance.

And then she heard his low, anguished cry. "*I can't.*" The words seemed torn from him, and the same force then launched him out of bed and had him pounding the wall with his fist, his erection gone. "Goddammit, Eva, I can't."

"It's okay." She sat up, the sheet pulled up to her chin. She felt for him, and, yeah, she was disappointed, but it was hardly the end of the world. "Honestly, Tiger, it happens."

He made a scoffing noise, then seemed to deflate. He reached down and tugged on his briefs, then sat on the edge of the bed. "I should have told you. But I thought—well, with you I thought it would be okay. But it's not. Hell, I think it may actually be worse."

He met her eyes, and she couldn't find a single word. She was too confused. Too troubled by the way he seemed to be drowning in a pain that seemed bigger than the actual problem.

"I'm sorry," he said. Then he got up and left the room.

And since there was no way she was ending the conversation on that note, she slid out of bed, grabbed her robe from the hook on the closet door, and followed him into the living room.

She found him on the couch and settled in beside him, then put her hand gently on his knee. He turned to her, managed a tiny smile, and then slid his arm around her shoulder.

Relieved, she leaned against him, thankful that the huge gap that had filled the space between them in the bedroom seemed to have disappeared. But she couldn't let it go. She knew she ought to be hurt by his words—how did she make it worse?—but mostly she was worried about him.

She needed to understand, and he was the only one who could explain it to her. And at the risk of bringing it all back to the surface, she dove back into the quagmire, and asked him very softly to tell her what was going on.

For a moment, he said nothing, and she thought he was going to ignore her. Then, slowly, he began to speak. "I've dated three women in the seven years since Teiko died," he said, obviously considering each word. "Not so much because I wanted to, but friends thought I shouldn't be alone. And, honestly, *dating* isn't entirely accurate. We went out a few times. Played the get-to-know-you game."

"And sex," she guessed.

He nodded. "Sometimes it's just about the contact. The connection. Even if there's nothing real underneath."

"I know. I get it."

"I got it, too. So did they. We just wanted— release." He let out a frustrated breath. "Which they got, but I didn't. Since she died—since I lost Teiko—I haven't been able to really make love to a woman, and no pill, no toy, no special oil advertised on the internet makes any difference at all."

"I'm sorry. I'm sure that's horribly frustrating. But if you're worried about the way I feel, you don't have to be. I just want you beside me. Don't get me wrong, it would be nice—I remember how nice it was—but mostly I just want to be with you. The intimacy of us."

He bent and kissed her head. "Baby, I—I know. And I believe you. And honestly, I would have told you before except that I thought it would be better with you."

"And instead it was worse."

He nodded.

"You loved her very much," she said. "It's hard to let go of someone you love."

His eyes widened in surprise. "How did you—"

She pressed a finger to his lips. "It's not exactly a secret that you loved her. That you still love her. And I guess it only makes sense that it's going to come out the most in the bedroom."

"I'm sorry," he said again.

"Please. Do not apologize for loving your wife. Never apologize for that."

He bent over and gently kissed her forehead, his arm tight around her.

"I do have one question," she admitted. "Why did

you think it would be better with me? And then why was it worse?"

"Don't you know?"

She shook her head. "That's why I'm asking."

"Same answer, both questions."

She just looked at him, silently urging him to tell her.

"It's because I love you."

Chapter Fifteen

EVA WISHED she had some sort of magic pill to give Tyree that would cure his guilt. She understood him loving his wife, and she certainly didn't begrudge him those feelings. But she hated knowing that he was having such a hard time moving forward, especially after so much time.

More than that, she hated the tiny insecurities that popped up inside herself. Because the truth was, she was falling back in love with him. Assuming she'd ever fallen out of love in the first place. And though he said he loved her, she feared that he really didn't. Or, more accurately, that he was holding back. That he wasn't willing to really be with her, because he feared that somehow taking a step toward her meant walking away from Teiko.

And, she supposed, it did. But wasn't that okay? Wasn't that the nature of healing?

Or was she being selfish, wishing that he'd heal faster and feel differently because that was what she wanted, not necessarily what he needed?

Honestly? She didn't know what to think.

And so she told herself that she wasn't going to think at all. She was in Austin for the time being, and she was going to do her work, spend time with her daughter, and enjoy as much time and intimacy with Tyree as he and their schedules would allow.

After that, she'd see where they stood. Maybe not the best plan, but her only other option was to put on the brakes and revert to simply co-parenting Elena.

Frankly, she'd moved way past that option.

Last night, he'd left the apartment before Elena had gotten home. They hadn't returned to the bedroom, but had instead snuggled on the couch, talking and making out as if they were teenagers. It had been sweet, and even a little refreshing, and the only downside was that she hadn't woken up in his arms.

They had, however, planned to meet for coffee, a walk around the lake, and then a leisurely breakfast. Which was why she was currently hanging out on the corner of Cesar Chavez and Congress, taking random pictures of the scenery just to pass the time.

Then her camera caught him walking up the trail holding two to-go cups and a white paper bag. She took a series of shots, him closer in each one, until finally only the coffee filled the frame. "It'll be great art," she said, when she lowered the camera to face his amused expression. "Or just something silly for me to look at when I'm alone."

"I vote the latter," he said, then passed her a coffee. "And I know we talked about getting breakfast, but it's such a gorgeous morning, I thought we might walk longer and have Kolaches." He held up the bag, and she peered in to find a selection of cheese, fruit, and sausage pastries.

Already hungry, she took out a sausage-filled one and took a bite, enjoying the sharp tang of the pastry-wrapped sausage. "This is great," she said. "Thanks."

"I also thought that if you wanted, we could spend the day together. Maybe head over to my house after our walk. Talk a bit. Fix some lunch. I have a covered patio and a great selection of wine. We could get a little drunk in the afternoon, see where it leads."

She shot him a sideways glance, wondering how far he intended it to lead. Another try after last night? Or did he want to back off the bedroom for a bit? Either way, though, it sounded tempting. And she could talk to him about her fears about his wifely guilt later. No sense ruining a perfectly lovely day with serious relationship talk.

"That sounds great. But are you sure it's a good idea? I've been usurping a lot of your time lately. What are your partners at The Fix going to think?"

"Probably that I'm ridiculously fond of you. And

that I haven't given myself a vacation in a long, long time."

"Is that what I am? A vacation?"

He popped the last bite of his pastry in his mouth, then took her hand. "You're a hell of a lot more than that," he said, with such sincerity it made her heart swell. "But speaking of vacations," he continued, "are you regretting not going to Vancouver?"

"Only as far as the temperature and humidity goes," she admitted. "It's brutal here. But the other amenities in Austin make up for it."

"Yeah?" he teased. "Like what?"

"Oh, you know. Great local bars. Cute guys on the jogging trails. Lots of places that serve breakfast tacos. General Austin stuff."

He tugged her to a stop, then kissed her, his mouth tasting like sausage. "That's all?"

"Oh, wait. There's this man I'm fond of…"

He laughed, and they continued along the walking path, chatting about the bar, the kids, the weather. Pretty much everything until she circled back to their original conversation. "I just want to be sure that I'm not a distraction. I know the idea is for you to up the revenue at the bar. I don't want to feel like I'm hindering that."

"You're not. And I like the distraction. It feels good, actually. Like I'm finding my center again."

She paused on the trail. "Do you mean that?"

He nodded. "Yeah. I do."

A smile tugged at her mouth. "In that case, good."

"Come on. Let's head back to my car."

They turned around, then headed back the way they came, foregoing the longer path that circled the downtown section of the river. "Can I ask you something else?" she asked after they'd walked about a quarter of a mile. "Why didn't you ever look for me? I mean, I know you sent letters, and since my father hid them, I never answered you. But why didn't you come looking for me to ask why?"

It wasn't until the words were out that she realized how much his answer mattered to her. And when he spoke, the words hit her with the force of a brick.

"I did," he said. "I saw you with David. And with Elena. I assumed she was his."

She stopped on the track, staring at him. "But that would mean I would have had to have hooked up with David about fifteen seconds after you shipped out."

"I know," he said, and she froze, stopped cold by the pain in his voice.

"Oh, Tiger," she said. "All these years, you'd thought—"

He shook his head, his finger on her lips gently silencing her. "You're here now. And none of that matters anymore."

Chapter Sixteen

IT WAS, Tyree thought, an entirely different vibe to be in the back bar waiting for his cue to strut than it was to be standing near the stage waiting for the contestants to start strutting.

All things being equal, he'd rather be in the audience. And for a moment, he wondered what the hell he'd been thinking. After all, the owner of the bar holding the contest didn't actually need to be *in* the contest. Surely that was some sort of horrible conflict of interest. Clearly, he'd been suffering from a particularly virulent form of insanity when he'd agreed.

Which, he supposed, was somewhat true. Because Eva did make him crazy, in the best possible way. And she was the one who'd roped him into this.

He fully intended to make her pay. In, of course, the best possible way. And detailed, sensual visions of the actual payment he planned to demand flitted through his mind in such vivid detail that he actually missed his cue to go on stage.

"Go!" Mina gave him a shove, and he stumbled forward as the emcee, Beverly, called to the crowd for a shout-out.

"Yes, folks, we finally did it! We finally convinced our very own Tyree Johnson to enter the contest. As you probably know, Tyree is your gracious host here at The Fix, and from what I understand, it took more than a little cajoling to get him on stage. But now it's time for the real test," she said, as a classic stripper tune started coming out of the speakers. "Come on, my friend, let's see those pecs."

He wasn't sure if he wanted to laugh, run, or find Eva and drag her up on the stage beside him. But he did find her in the crowd with Elena at her side, both of them looking ridiculously amused. Oh, yeah. There would most definitely be payment tonight.

The crowd started to urge him on, and what the hell, right? He could hardly ask dozens of men— including some of his own employees—to do what he didn't have the balls to do. Besides, he worked out. He might be forty-six, but he wasn't shabby.

With one quick motion, he grabbed the hem of his shirt and pulled it over his head, then tossed the T-shirt into the crowd, to a chorus of whoops and claps.

He struck a Mr. Universe-style pose, did a turn to show off his back, and then slid out of the spotlight to stand among the other tributes to the fires of insanity. Finally, he caught Eva's eye in the crowd, then chuckled when she fanned her face, as if to suggest that he was just too hot. Beside her, Elena had her hand over her mouth, obviously holding in laughter.

He bit back his own grin, feeling a bit like a fool, but having a lot more fun than he'd anticipated.

There was only one contestant after him, so he didn't have long to wait until all the men on the stage were released to mingle in the crowd. He searched for Eva, but realized that she'd disappeared in the crush. That was also the moment he realized that his spur of the moment decision to toss his shirt into the crowd had been a boneheaded move. Apparently, he was going to have to mingle half-naked with his customers.

Great.

"Hey there, stud." Eva's sultry voice teased him from behind. "I've got something for you."

He turned to find her holding out a black *The Fix on Sixth* T-shirt for him.

"Have I told you how very incredibly wonderful you are?"

"Feel free to fill me in. Although this is more self-ishness than awesomeness. It's in my interest to cover you up, after all. It's one thing on stage. Entirely another to be walking around in the wild where other women can ogle you."

"Ogle? Hmm. Sounds kinky." He stepped closer

and put his arms around her waist. "Maybe later we can do some ogling."

"Okay, you two," Elena said as she approached. "Break it up."

"Nothing doing," Tyree said. And then, because he was still on his celebrity high, he pulled Eva to him and kissed her long and hard, not releasing her until he heard he sounds of cheers and applause from all around them.

When he did let her go, she laughed, a little breathless. "If that's your definition of ogling, I'm all for a little more. But what—"

Her question was cut off by Beverly's return to the stage. "After this, I'm taking you to the Driskill," he whispered, causing Eva to turn in his arms.

"You better not mean just for a drink," she said.

"Third floor. A lovely room. I'm assured by the front desk that it even has a bed."

"In other words, all the amenities we need."

"In other words," he added, "no kids in second bedrooms."

Beside them, one of the kids in question was jumping up and down, and it took Tyree a second to wrap is mind around what she was saying.

"You won! You won! Dad! Hello? *Daddy*! You won!"

And in that moment, he realized two things. First, that his chest was going to be plastered on the pages of his own damn calendar.

And second, that for the first time, his daughter had called him Dad.

HE HADN'T BEEN LYING when he told her it was a lovely room. It was stunning. Well-appointed. Comfortable. Altogether fabulous.

And Tyree couldn't care less.

All he wanted—all he needed—was Eva. She'd become the center of his world, the focal point of his days and his nights.

She was the mother of his daughter. His friend. His lover.

And, dammit, it was the last part that he intended to explore tonight. *Had* to. Because he'd been craving her all damn day. The simple, attractive T-shirt. The thin, summer skirt. The casual sandals. She looked like a picnic, and he wanted to devour her.

"Bed," he said, the moment they entered the room.

She lifted her brows. "Bossy."

"Oh, yes," he said, then scooped her up and tossed her where he wanted her, making her squeal with laughter—a laughter he quickly turned into a sensual groan when he lifted her skirt and tugged down her panties, then dipped his head for a deliciously intimate taste.

"Oh, God," she cried, her hands clutching his

head, her hips bucking against his mouth. He'd planned on a soft, romantic night. Instead, this was hard and hot and wild—and he couldn't deny that he liked it. The taste of her, the need. The hot, shameless way she demanded his fingers and tongue.

And, dear Lord, his cock liked it, too. He was hard. Painfully so. And he wanted so badly to sink inside of her.

He knew better, though. He didn't want a repeat of the other night. All he wanted tonight was pleasure. All he wanted was to see her wild for him, to hear her cry his name. To make her shatter in his arms.

He teased her clit and her pussy mercilessly, and he could feel the tension building inside her, making her climb higher and higher. And it was him taking her there. The power of that humbled him, knowing that he was bringing her such pleasure. Knowing that they could share such incredibly intimacy.

And there it was.

He wanted that. The sharing. He wanted to feel her tighten around his cock. He wanted her to milk him, to go over the edge with him.

He wanted that—he did, dammit.

And before he could talk himself out of trying, he stripped off his jeans, then slid on top of her. His mouth found hers as he straddled her, pushing her knees up to open her even more too him.

"Tyree, are you sure?"

But he didn't answer her with words. He just slid his fingers inside her, making sure she was wet enough for him, ready enough. And then he slowly thrust his cock into her. Just a little, just a test. But it was good— oh, Christ, it was good—then a little more and a little more until finally he was pistoning against her, their bodies slapping together, and she was crying out, telling him how good it felt, how deep he was, how she never wanted him to stop.

And he was close, so damn close. So was she, her muscles clenching around him, taking him further and further until finally his entire body shattered, the force of his orgasm ripping him apart as intense waves of joy shook him. Joy. Pleasure. Passion.

Eva.

It was all Eva. Every thought. Every feeling. Every wild sensation.

She filled him. Illuminated him. Made him whole.

He wanted her. Needed her.

For one short moment, he reveled in that simple truth. Then everything imploded, and reality hauled back and kicked him hard in the balls.

A shudder cut through him, and he pulled out of her as a tidal wave of heavy, potent guilt crashed over him, sweeping him away. Sweeping everything away. Until he was lost. So damn lost.

"Tyree?" She sat up, confusion flooding her voice. "Are you okay?"

Christ, he probably looked like he'd had a stroke.

He held up a hand to stave off her touch. "Fine," he said. "I'm—"

Lost? Guilty? Confused? Pitiful?

He didn't know. Dear Lord, he didn't know.

"I'm sorry," he said as he slid off the bed. It was all he could say.

It was the best he could do.

And though she begged him to stop, to stay, to explain, he just moved faster, hurrying into his clothes and then out the door into the Driskill's abandoned hallway and the illusion that he'd gotten his shit under control.

Chapter Seventeen

"I DON'T KNOW, MOM," Elena said, fidgeting with her phone as she perched on the bed Eva had been using. "I still think you're being a little hasty."

Eva frowned as she turned a circle in the room, checking to make sure she'd tossed all her personal things into her duffel. Eva had returned to the apartment in the middle of the night, then waited up for Elena to come home. They'd talked on the couch for hours, and Eva had explained to her daughter that she needed to go back to San Diego. Not only because she had a business to run, but because Tyree needed space.

"I'm not saying it's over." *Please, don't let it be over.* "But I am saying he has some things to work out."

"Then work them out with him. I mean, come on, Mom. This is my dad."

Eva sighed, and stopped packing, her attention

focused entirely on her daughter. "I know. And I know that you'd thought you were getting the fairy tale. Honestly, I thought I was, too. But that's not the way the story's turning out. Your father loved his wife. Really loved her. And that's wonderful, but it's also confusing for him. And it only makes it harder for him when I'm here."

"Sounds like a cop-out to me."

Eva shook her head. "No. No, it's not like that. I don't want to leave. I love him. I love him more than I did before you were born, and there's not much I wouldn't give to stay here with him."

"Then stay." Elena wasn't crying, but her voice sounded thick with coming tears.

"I said there wasn't much. But I won't give myself. I won't settle. I did that before, and I'm not going to do it again."

Elena licked her lips. "But it's Daddy."

"Oh, baby," Eva said, as she lifted the duffel onto her shoulder. "Whatever Tyree Johnson is to me, I swear he will always be your daddy."

A tear trickled from her daughter's eye, and Eva forced herself to stay strong. She leaned over and kissed her forehead. "I'm going now," she said, then hurried into the living room and toward the front door, intending to go down to the street and wait for her ride share.

Instead, she opened the door and found Tyree.

"You're leaving?"

Eva turned, shooting a frustrated glance toward the bedroom. And toward the daughter inside who'd been fiddling—apparently texting—on her phone.

"We both know it's best, Tyree. And it doesn't have to be goodbye. We can talk later. But you need space."

He stepped into the apartment, forcing her to either hold her ground or take a step back. She stepped back. It was just too damn hard to think when he was that near.

"Don't tell me what I need. Especially when what I need is you."

"Do you?"

"Eva…" His voice sounded ripped. Like by just asking the question she'd broken his heart.

She drew in a breath, determined to remain firm. "Fine, maybe you don't need space, but I do. I need time. I think we both do."

He took her hand, and she felt it swallowed up in the warmth of his strong grip. "Please, Eva. I don't want to lose you."

"I don't want to lose you either," she said, then saw his shoulders sag with relief. "But I'm not going to settle anymore, either." She drew in a breath for courage. "I have a career I love back in California, and I want a man who loves me. Who isn't afraid to love me completely."

She touched her fingertips to his face. "I don't know if that's you or not, Tiger. I'd like to believe it is.

But you won't let yourself love me. Not fully. Because you think it's dishonoring Teiko. You're a big man, Ty, with a big heart. Did you ever think there's room in there for the both of us?"

"Eva, please."

But she just shook her head. "No. I'm sorry. I have to go home. Tell Jenna I'll call her. I can come out and do all the calendar shots right after Mr. December is chosen. I'll make it work. And Elena can do the publicity shots and I'll clean them up in Photoshop for her."

He rubbed his eyebrow, his expression pained. "Don't go. Can't we—"

"There's no *we*," she said gently. "There can't be a *we* until you figure some things out."

She kissed him gently on the cheek. "I love you," she said. "For that matter, I never stopped loving you. And I never will. But right now, I have to go."

Chapter Eighteen

OVER TWO MILLION people lived in the Austin metropolitan area, but with each passing day without Eva, the town felt more and more empty. Hollow.

Tyree sighed. It wasn't the town, he thought, as he stood at the front window of The Fix and looked out at the dense crowd of people out for a good time on a Saturday night. It was her. Because any place without Eva was a cold, empty space.

Frustrated, he pulled out his phone, just as he'd done every few hours for the last three days. This time, though, he was finally going to call her.

Except when he dialed, it was Elena's number.

She answered on the first ring. "Hey, Daddy. You okay?"

He bit back a sad smile. Already, the kid knew him too well. "Fine," he lied. "Listen, Eli's studying late at a friend's, and you and I both have the night off from The Fix. Want to grab dinner with me?"

"You're not working tonight?"

"Nope." He justified the lie by reminding himself that he'd tell Reece to take over and walk out that door the minute she agreed to meet him.

"Um, Daddy?"

"Yeah?"

"Turn around."

Shit. He did, then found himself facing his daughter, who sat having a drink at one of the tables in the far corner of the main room, with Amanda, Nolan, and Shelby sitting beside her.

"Well, what do you know," he said. "Looks like we both hang out at the same place on our day off."

Even across the room, he could see her roll her eyes. Then she said something to the others, stood up, and very deliberately walked over to him, ending the call in the process.

"So, I'm guessing this is a yes for dinner?"

She crossed her arms and cocked her head. "You know I'm not the one you want to be having dinner with. Call her."

He shook his head, then sighed. "She has her life out there."

"Yeah. But she doesn't have you."

"Have you talked to her?"

"Well, duh. She's my mom."

"And?"

"And you already know. She loves you. She's not the problem here. I thought she was before she took off, but we've talked some more and I've thought a lot about it. And she's right. You're the one who needs to kick his own ass."

He fought back a bitter laugh. Wasn't that the truth?

She leaned in and kissed his cheek. "I'm sorry, Daddy, but I've already got dinner plans. And honestly? I think you need to sit down and do some serious thinking. You're throwing away happiness and thinking it makes you a martyr. It doesn't. It just makes you stupid."

"That's harsh," he said.

She lifted a shoulder. "Maybe. But it sure looks like truth from where I'm standing."

TYREE WAS DOZING on the couch when Eli walked in. He did a lot of that lately. Either slept or buried himself in work. There really wasn't much of a middle ground.

"You're home," Eli said as Tyree scrubbed his face with his palms, trying to wake up. His beard, which he usually kept trimmed, had grown wild. Right at the moment, he really didn't care.

Eli plunked down on the coffee table right in front of him. "You look like crap."

"And a warm welcome to you, too, son."

"At least you've got your sense of humor."

Tyree didn't answer. He wasn't sure he had any sense of humor left, actually.

"Elena picked me up after school today," he said. "We went to Starbucks."

"How is she?"

"Better than you, that's for damn sure."

"Language, Eli."

"Damn, fuck, shit, piss."

Tyree opened his eyes wide. "What the devil's wrong with you?"

"There." Eli pointed a finger at him. "That's the question. What's wrong with *you?*"

Tyree drew in one long breath, then let it out slowly. "I'm in a funk. I know it, but I'll get out of it. I just need a little time. A little space. Everyone needs a little space sometimes."

"Elena says you need a kick in the balls."

The words almost made him smile. Instead, he said, "Let's temporarily remove your sister from the role-model list, okay?"

"Do you remember the last time we went to Mom's grave?"

Tyree's head whipped up, both at the mention of Teiko and at the complete non sequitur. "Of course. That was the seventh anniversary of her death."

"No," Eli said. "No more of that shit."

The words stung. More than that, they confused. "What are you talking about?"

"Anniversaries are for celebrating. I'm not gonna celebrate losing my mom. Not anymore."

"Eli—"

"No. Listen to me. I'm not going there anymore. Not like that, anyway. Not like it's a ritual."

"Be careful, son." Tyree's whole body felt cold. Tense. "You're treading on very thin ice."

"I've been thinking about it. I don't think she'd like it. I remember her every day, Dad," he said, his eyes shining now. "I don't have to go to a grave to do that. And you know what? She wouldn't want me to."

A tear trickled down the side of his nose. "She'd tell me I was rearranging my life for a life that didn't exist anymore. She'd want me to stop. Like with my jeans."

He'd been about to explode. Now he felt deflated and confused. "Jeans?"

"Yeah." Eli nodded. "You said she wouldn't care what I wore that day, remember? And you were right. She doesn't care what we wear, Dad. She just wants us to be happy."

Tyree sat for a second, his eyes unnaturally wide, fighting his own urge to cry.

"You aren't happy, Dad."

And, dammit, there went the tears. He drew in a wet, stuttering breath. "It's not you, son. You know that, right? You're the best thing in my life. You and Elena."

"Yeah, yeah. I get that. So does she. But Dad, come on. It's kind of obvious. And you know what? Mom would get it, too."

For a moment, Tyree simply sat there. A little shell-shocked, the world feeling hollow around him, muffled. Like the eerie silence after an explosion. Then he drew in a breath, gathered himself, and faced his son. "I think your mom would have liked Eva."

The corner of Eli's mouth twitched. "Yeah. Me, too."

He thought about Eva. About the life she had in San Diego. About how he must somehow convince her that things had changed. That he loved her fully and completely and without reservation. That he wasn't going to give up on them, no matter what the price and no matter how long it took to prove it to her.

Then he looked at his son. "Did you mean what you said the first time we had Elena and Eva over to the house? About thinking it would be cool to live in California?"

"Are you kidding? Surfing? Hell, yeah."

Tyree nodded, considering.

"So, I guess you're going to have to go see her now, huh?"

"I guess I am." He looked at his son, seeing a

much older and wiser kid than he had the day before. "How'd you get to be so smart, anyway?

"Must've got it from Mom," Eli said, dropping to the couch and letting Tyree swing an arm around his shoulder. "'Cause you can be a real dumb ass."

Chapter Nineteen

THANK goodness Eva's work schedule was light, because ever since she'd returned to San Diego, she'd had the most terrible time concentrating.

Fortunately, Marianne had taken point. Taking over organizing the calendar, covering a few basic shoots for corporate clients, and handling the various retouching orders that had come in from past weddings, parties, and the like. Eva had trained Marianne on Photoshop years ago, and she was patting herself on the back for having made that decision.

Now, Eva was staring at her own computer screen trying to organize her upcoming schedule. She'd talked to Jenna yesterday, and they'd agreed that she'd fly to Austin in July for a two-day shoot, then again when the contest ended in early October. That way they could be sure and have the template for the calendar worked out by the time it needed to go to press.

Already, Eva was nervous about the trip. She hadn't heard from Tyree, and was desperately afraid that she'd pushed too hard. He'd loved Teiko so much, and she knew that his wife's death had almost broken him.

Had she been an idiot to push him? She didn't know. All she knew was that she couldn't share a bed with a man who felt guilty when he made love to her.

No. She hadn't made the wrong choice. It was the right one, absolutely.

But it was also the choice that hurt.

She heard the *beep beep beep* of someone punching in the code for the studio's keypad lock, and she moaned in anticipation. Marianne had promised to return with a Starbucks latte, and Eva was in desperate need of the caffeine.

"You saved me," she called. "Hurry up and get in here before I pass out."

"Wouldn't want that."

She gasped, her hand flying to her chest and her heart pounding as Tyree stepped into her doorway, then leaned casually against the frame.

"I—What are you doing here? And how did you get in?"

"Elena told me the code. Why are you going to pass out?"

"Shock, apparently," she retorted. "Seriously, why are you here?"

"Do you want the long answer or the short one?"

She considered, decided to go for the gold. "The short one."

"Because I love you," he said, the words like the sweetest perfume. "Because I need you. And because I've finally got my shit together."

"Oh." Butterflies fluttered in her stomach as her pulse skittered. "And the long version?"

"That I'm not going to lose you. That I'll do whatever it takes, for however long it takes, including moving back to San Diego if you need more time to believe that I mean it, or if you don't want to leave your home or your job. I already lost one woman I love, Eva. I'm not going to lose you, too. And I'm not going to feel guilty about loving you. It's not fair to you, and it's not fair to Teiko.

That surprised her. "Not fair to her?"

"She wasn't a bitch," he said. "She'd want me to be happy."

"I think I would have liked her."

"You would have. But she's my past. You're my present. And my future. At least," he added, "I hope you are."

She came around the desk slowly, then stood right in front of him and took his hands, forcing herself not to simply leap into his arms. It was important to do this right.

"Definitely the future," she said. "But there are three legs to this stool, Tyree."

His brow furrowed in confusion.

"You love me. You love Teiko. And you love The Fix."

"True?" He said the word, but his tone and his expression turned it into a question.

"I told you I'd never expect you to stop loving her. And you damn sure better not stop loving me. But if you think that I want you to leave The Fix behind, you're sorely mistaken."

"I can't ask you to pick up and move to Austin."

She nodded. "Yeah, you can. You need a whole building. I just need my camera." She made a face. "Well, and Marianne. But she can be my West Coast office, and I can fly here when I need to." She grinned. "See? I hook up with you and suddenly even my career has more cachet. And you forget that my daughter's there."

He chuckled. "Fair enough. Although Eli will be disappointed."

Her brows rose.

"He was looking forward to learning to surf. I figure he'll get over it."

"So we'll go back?" She couldn't wait. She missed Elena and the friends she'd made at The Fix more than she'd anticipated. And though she loved Marianne, they'd still talk every day by phone or by text.

And her friend would love being in charge of Eva's West Coast division.

"We'll go back," he agreed. "But in a few days."

"Oh?" She lifted her brows. "And what exactly will we be doing in all that extra time?"

He laughed. "That, yes. But I also want to walk around San Diego with you. Visit the places we used to go. I want to stroll hand in hand with the woman I love, and I want to soak up this town. Mostly, I want to remember us."

"Us," she repeated. "I like the sound of that."

"So do I," he said, then kissed her. A long, sweet kiss full of passion and promise. A kiss that sealed the past and opened the door on a future.

Their future. Together. As a family.

Epilogue

MEGAN CLARK PACED the reception area of PCM Enterprises, still unable to believe she'd made such a boneheaded mistake. And she had absolutely no one to blame but herself.

Well, herself and Parker Manning's idiot assistant.

But, no. Megan couldn't pass the buck to the other woman. This had been her project, her baby, her stupid, lame-ass mistake.

All she'd wanted to do was prove to the folks at The Fix that Jenna hadn't made a mistake in hiring her. That she actually had a brain and could help out with all of the various tasks at the popular bar. Most important, she wanted to help out with the marketing, because that was Jenna's area, and Jenna had taken a risk and offered Megan a job, even though The Fix was on a tight budget. And even though Megan knew buckets about makeup but next to nothing about marketing.

Still, she was the one who'd come up with the idea to start advertising the entrants in the Man of the Month contest instead of just the winner. Get people excited to see who was competing against each other.

And she was the one who'd wanted to up the game a bit where the entrants were concerned. Yes, most of the guys who entered were total hotties, but very few of them were local celebrities. Which meant that very few people were paying attention. But if they could get some of the local television guys or wealthy business owners … basically anyone who made the news or the tabloids regularly, that would be a total plus. Especially if the guy was a social media draw.

And Parker Manning was about as social media centric as they came.

He came from a Texas oil money family, but he'd lived in LA for a while. He'd dated actresses, dabbled in producing, and been front and center with two successful companies that he'd turned around and sold right after they hit big.

Rumor had it he'd tripled his net worth within a year, and the starting number in his family trust fund had been none-too-shabby.

Everyone at The Fix had agreed that he'd be a great guy to have on the contest slate, and since he and Megan had run in the same circles in LA, she'd assured Jenna she could land him.

In fact, she'd not only run in the same circles, she'd actually crossed his path. Once, he'd even asked her out, making clear that he was very, very interested. She'd been tempted. He had a bad boy reputation, so he wasn't a guy she'd want to date, but back in LA she'd been wilder and stupider, and there'd been a definite tug in the area of her nether regions.

She hadn't accepted his offer, though. That was about the time she'd started dating Carlton. And he'd made it very clear that she was his exclusive property.

She shivered, remembering those months with him. Remembering more why she'd bolted.

She'd left Los Angeles without looking back, and her first sight of Parker in Austin had been an unpleasant twinge. That was part of why she hadn't asked him to participate personally the first time. She'd put the request out through his assistant, who'd told Megan that Parker would love to be part of it.

But apparently his former assistant was a space cadet—and Megan was a stupid idiot for not making sure the signed agreement had been returned.

Now Parker was pissed because his picture was on flyers for a contest he knew nothing about, and Megan had to somehow dig herself out of this hole.

She had no idea how she was going to manage that. She hoped their past acquaintance would smooth the way. And groveling was definitely on the menu.

"Ms. Clark?"

At the sound of her name, Megan stopped pacing, probably to the great relief of the overly coiffed receptionist.

"Yes?"

"Mr. Manning will see you now. If you'll just follow me?"

She drew in a deep breath, then nodded as she fell in step behind the leggy blonde. Parker's office was down the hall. A corner office, of course, and when the receptionist opened the door, Megan was struck by the stunning view of the Capitol building, the University tower, and a wide spread of the Austin skyline.

More than that, though, she was struck by the sight of the man who stood in front of his desk, leaning casually against it in a light gray suit that looked like it cost more than she made in a year. Possibly two.

His eyes met hers, an icy blue that somehow radiated heat.

"Ms. Clark," he said, his voice a sensual tease. "I understand we have a little problem."

"I—well, yes." She sounded like an idiot, but dear God, he was distracting.

His eyes swept over her in an inspection so slow and intimate it left her with the distinct impression that he'd seen right through her simple black dress. "Fortunately, I have a solution."

"Oh," she said. "Um, what?"

That wide, sensual mouth curved up with obvious amusement. "I thought that would've been obvious, Megan. I want you."

The Men of Man of the Month!

Are you eager to learn which Man of the Month book features which sexy hero? Here's a handy list!

Down On Me - meet Reece
Hold On Tight - meet Spencer
Need You Now - meet Cameron
Start Me Up - meet Nolan
Get It On - meet Tyree
In Your Eyes - meet Parker
Turn Me On - meet Derek
Shake It Up - meet Landon
All Night Long - meet Easton
In Too Deep - meet Matthew
Light My Fire - meet Griffin
Walk The Line - meet Brent
&
Bar Bites: A Man of the Month Cookbook

Down On Me excerpt

Did you miss book one in the Man of the Month series? Here's an excerpt from Down On Me!

Chapter One

Reece Walker ran his palms over the slick, soapy ass of the woman in his arms and knew that he was going straight to hell.

Not because he'd slept with a woman he barely knew. Not because he'd enticed her into bed with a series of well-timed bourbons and particularly inventive half-truths. Not even because he'd lied to his best friend Brent about why Reece couldn't drive with him to the airport to pick up Jenna, the third player in their trifecta of lifelong friendship.

No, Reece was staring at the fiery pit because he was a lame, horny asshole without the balls to tell the naked beauty standing in the shower with him that she wasn't the woman he'd been thinking about for the last four hours.

And if that wasn't one of the pathways to hell, it damn sure ought to be.

He let out a sigh of frustration, and Megan tilted her head, one eyebrow rising in question as she slid her hand down to stroke his cock, which was demonstrating no guilt whatsoever about the whole going to hell issue. "Am I boring you?"

"Hardly." That, at least, was the truth. He felt like a prick, yes. But he was a well-satisfied one. "I was just thinking that you're beautiful."

She smiled, looking both shy and pleased—and Reece felt even more like a heel. What the devil was wrong with him? She *was* beautiful. And hot and funny and easy to talk to. Not to mention good in bed.

But she wasn't Jenna, which was a ridiculous comparison. Because Megan qualified as fair game, whereas Jenna was one of his two best friends. She trusted him. Loved him. And despite the way his cock perked up at the thought of doing all sorts of delicious things with her in bed, Reece knew damn well that would never happen. No way was he risking their friendship. Besides, Jenna didn't love him like that. Never had, never would.

And that—plus about a billion more reasons— meant that Jenna was entirely off-limits.

Too bad his vivid imagination hadn't yet gotten the memo.

Fuck it.

He tightened his grip, squeezing Megan's perfect rear. "Forget the shower," he murmured. "I'm taking you back to bed." He needed this. Wild. Hot. Demanding. And dirty enough to keep him from thinking.

Hell, he'd scorch the earth if that's what it took to burn Jenna from his mind—and he'd leave Megan limp, whimpering, and very, very satisfied. His guilt. Her pleasure. At least it would be a win for one of them.

And who knows? Maybe he'd manage to fuck the fantasies of his best friend right out of his head.

It didn't work.

Reece sprawled on his back, eyes closed, as Megan's gentle fingers traced the intricate outline of the tattoos inked across his pecs and down his arms. Her touch was warm and tender, in stark contrast to the way he'd just fucked her—a little too wild, a little too hard, as if he were fighting a battle, not making love.

Well, that was true, wasn't it?

But it was a battle he'd lost. Victory would have brought oblivion. Yet here he was, a naked woman beside him, and his thoughts still on Jenna, as wild and intense and impossible as they'd been since that night eight months ago when the earth had shifted beneath him, and he'd let himself look at her as a woman and not as a friend.

One breathtaking, transformative night, and Jenna didn't even realize it. And he'd be damned if he'd ever let her figure it out.

Beside him, Megan continued her exploration, one fingertip tracing the outline of a star. "No names? No wife or girlfriend's initials hidden in the design?"

He turned his head sharply, and she burst out laughing.

"Oh, don't look at me like that." She pulled the sheet up to cover her breasts as she rose to her knees beside him. "I'm just making conversation. No hidden agenda at all. Believe me, the last thing I'm interested in is a relationship." She scooted away, then sat on the edge of the bed, giving him an enticing view of her bare back. "I don't even do overnights."

As if to prove her point, she bent over, grabbed her bra off the floor, and started getting dressed.

"Then that's one more thing we have in common." He pushed himself up, rested his back against the headboard, and enjoyed the view as she wiggled into her jeans.

"Good," she said, with such force that he knew she meant it, and for a moment he wondered what had soured her on relationships.

As for himself, he hadn't soured so much as fizzled. He'd had a few serious girlfriends over the years, but it never worked out. No matter how good it started, invariably the relationship crumbled. Eventually, he had to acknowledge that he simply wasn't relationship material. But that didn't mean he was a monk, the last eight months notwithstanding.

She put on her blouse and glanced around, then slipped her feet into her shoes. Taking the hint, he got up and pulled on his jeans and T-shirt. "Yes?" he asked, noticing the way she was eying him speculatively.

"The truth is, I was starting to think you might be in a relationship."

"What? Why?"

She shrugged. "You were so quiet there for a while, I wondered if maybe I'd misjudged you. I thought you might be married and feeling guilty."

Guilty.

The word rattled around in his head, and he groaned. "Yeah, you could say that."

"Oh, *hell*. Seriously?"

"No," he said hurriedly. "Not that. I'm not cheating on my non-existent wife. I wouldn't. Not ever." Not in small part because Reece wouldn't ever have a wife since he thought the institution of marriage was a crock, but he didn't see the need to explain that to Megan.

"But as for guilt?" he continued. "Yeah, tonight I've got that in spades."

She relaxed slightly. "Hmm. Well, sorry about the guilt, but I'm glad about the rest. I have rules, and I consider myself a good judge of character. It makes me cranky when I'm wrong."

"Wouldn't want to make you cranky."

"Oh, you really wouldn't. I can be a total bitch." She sat on the edge of the bed and watched as he tugged on his boots. "But if you're not hiding a wife in your attic, what are you feeling guilty about? I assure you, if it has anything to do with my satisfaction, you needn't feel guilty at all." She flashed a mischievous grin, and he couldn't help but smile back. He hadn't invited a woman into his bed for eight long months. At least he'd had the good fortune to pick one he actually liked.

"It's just that I'm a crappy friend," he admitted.

"I doubt that's true."

"Oh, it is," he assured her as he tucked his wallet into his back pocket. The irony, of course, was that as far as Jenna knew, he was an excellent friend. The best. One of her two pseudo-brothers with whom she'd sworn a blood oath the summer after sixth grade, almost twenty years ago.

From Jenna's perspective, Reece was at least as good as Brent, even if the latter scored bonus points because he was picking Jenna up at the airport while Reece was trying to fuck his personal demons into oblivion. Trying anything, in fact, that would exorcise the memory of how she'd clung to him that night, her curves enticing and her breath intoxicating, and not just because of the scent of too much alcohol.

She'd trusted him to be the white knight, her noble rescuer, and all he'd been able to think about was the feel of her body, soft and warm against his, as he carried her up the stairs to her apartment.

A wild craving had hit him that night, like a tidal wave of emotion crashing over him, washing away the outer shell of friendship and leaving nothing but raw desire and a longing so potent it nearly brought him to his knees.

It had taken all his strength to keep his distance when the only thing he'd wanted was to cover every inch of her naked body with kisses. To stroke her skin and watch her writhe with pleasure.

He'd won a hard-fought battle when he reined in his desire that night. But his victory wasn't without its wounds. She'd pierced his heart when she'd drifted to sleep in his arms, whispering that she loved him—and he knew that she meant it only as a friend.

More than that, he knew that he was the biggest asshole to ever walk the earth.

Thankfully, Jenna remembered nothing of that night. The liquor had stolen her memories, leaving her with a monster hangover, and him with a Jenna-shaped hole in his heart.

"Well?" Megan pressed. "Are you going to tell me? Or do I have to guess?"

"I blew off a friend."

"Yeah? That probably won't score you points in the Friend of the Year competition, but it doesn't sound too dire. Unless you were the best man and blew off the wedding? Left someone stranded at the side of the road somewhere in West Texas? Or promised to feed their cat and totally forgot? Oh, God. Please tell me you didn't kill Fluffy."

He bit back a laugh, feeling slightly better. "A friend came in tonight, and I feel like a complete shit for not meeting her plane."

"Well, there are taxis. And I assume she's an adult?"

"She is, and another friend is there to pick her up."

"I see," she said, and the way she slowly nodded suggested that she saw too much. "I'm guessing that *friend* means *girlfriend*? Or, no. You wouldn't do that. So she must be an ex."

"Really not," he assured her. "Just a friend. Life-long, since sixth grade."

"Oh, I get it. Longtime friend. High expectations. She's going to be pissed."

"Nah. She's cool. Besides, she knows I usually work nights."

"Then what's the problem?"

He ran his hand over his shaved head, the bristles

from the day's growth like sandpaper against his palm. "Hell if I know," he lied, then forced a smile, because whether his problem was guilt or lust or just plain stupidity, she hardly deserved to be on the receiving end of his bullshit.

He rattled his car keys. "How about I buy you one last drink before I take you home?"

"You're sure you don't mind a working drink?" Reece asked as he helped Megan out of his cherished baby blue vintage Chevy pickup. "Normally I wouldn't take you to my job, but we just hired a new bar back, and I want to see how it's going."

He'd snagged one of the coveted parking spots on Sixth Street, about a block down from The Fix, and he glanced automatically toward the bar, the glow from the windows relaxing him. He didn't own the place, but it was like a second home to him and had been for one hell of a long time.

"There's a new guy in training, and you're not there? I thought you told me you were the manager?"

"I did, and I am, but Tyree's there. The owner, I mean. He's always on site when someone new is starting. Says it's his job, not mine. Besides, Sunday's my day off, and Tyree's a stickler for keeping to the schedule."

"Okay, but why are you going then?"

"Honestly? The new guy's my cousin. He'll prob-ably give me shit for checking in on him, but old habits die hard." Michael had been almost four when Vincent died, and the loss of his dad hit him hard. At sixteen, Reece had tried to be stoic, but Uncle Vincent had been like a second father to him, and he'd always thought of Mike as more brother than cousin. Either way, from that day on, he'd made it his job to watch out for the kid.

"Nah, he'll appreciate it," Megan said. "I've got a little sister, and she gripes when I check up on her, but it's all for show. She likes knowing I have her back. And as for getting a drink where you work, I don't mind at all."

As a general rule, late nights on Sunday were dead, both in the bar and on Sixth Street, the popular downtown Austin street that had been a focal point of the city's nightlife for decades. Tonight was no excep-tion. At half-past one in the morning, the street was mostly deserted. Just a few cars moving slowly, their headlights shining toward the west, and a smattering of couples, stumbling and laughing. Probably tourists on their way back to one of the downtown hotels.

It was late April, though, and the spring weather was drawing both locals and tourists. Soon, the area —and the bar—would be bursting at the seams. Even on a slow Sunday night.

Situated just a few blocks down from Congress Avenue, the main downtown artery, The Fix on Sixth attracted a healthy mix of tourists and locals. The bar had existed in one form or another for decades, becoming a local staple, albeit one that had been falling deeper and deeper into disrepair until Tyree had bought the place six years ago and started it on much-needed life support.

"You've never been here before?" Reece asked as he paused in front of the oak and glass doors etched with the bar's familiar logo.

"I only moved downtown last month. I was in Los Angeles before."

The words hit Reece with unexpected force. Jenna had been in LA, and a wave of both longing and regret crashed over him. He should have gone with Brent. What the hell kind of friend was he, punishing Jenna because he couldn't control his own damn libido?

With effort, he forced the thoughts back. He'd already beaten that horse to death.

"Come on," he said, sliding one arm around her shoulder and pulling open the door with his other. "You're going to love it."

He led her inside, breathing in the familiar mix of alcohol, southern cooking, and something indiscernible he liked to think of as the scent of a damn good time. As he expected, the place was mostly empty. There was no live music on Sunday nights, and at less than an hour to closing, there were only three customers in the front room.

"Megan, meet Cameron," Reece said, pulling out a stool for her as he nodded to the bartender in introduction. Down the bar, he saw Griffin Draper, a regular, lift his head, his face obscured by his hoodie, but his attention on Megan as she chatted with Cam about the house wines.

Reece nodded hello, but Griffin turned back to his notebook so smoothly and nonchalantly that Reece wondered if maybe he'd just been staring into space, thinking, and hadn't seen Reece or Megan at all. That was probably the case, actually. Griff wrote a popular podcast that had been turned into an even more popular web series, and when he wasn't recording the dialogue, he was usually writing a script.

"So where's Mike? With Tyree?"

Cameron made a face, looking younger than his twenty-four years. "Tyree's gone."

"You're kidding. Did something happen with Mike?" His cousin was a responsible kid. Surely he hadn't somehow screwed up his first day on the job.

"No, Mike's great." Cam slid a Scotch in front of Reece. "Sharp, quick, hard worker. He went off the clock about an hour ago, though. So you just missed him."

"Tyree shortened his shift?"

Cam shrugged. "Guess so. Was he supposed to be on until closing?"

"Yeah." Reece frowned. "He was. Tyree say why he cut him loose?"

"No, but don't sweat it. Your cousin's fitting right in. Probably just because it's Sunday and slow. " He made a face. "And since Tyree followed him out, guess who's closing for the first time alone."

"So you're in the hot seat, huh? " Reece tried to sound casual. He was standing behind Megan's stool, but now he moved to lean against the bar, hoping his casual posture suggested that he wasn't worried at all. He was, but he didn't want Cam to realize it. Tyree didn't leave employees to close on their own. Not until he'd spent weeks training them.

"I told him I want the weekend assistant manager position. I'm guessing this is his way of seeing how I work under pressure."

"Probably," Reece agreed half-heartedly. "What did he say?"

"Honestly, not much. He took a call in the office, told Mike he could head home, then about fifteen minutes later said he needed to take off, too, and that I was the man for the night."

"Trouble?" Megan asked.

"No. Just chatting up my boy," Reece said, surprised at how casual his voice sounded. Because the scenario had trouble printed all over it. He just wasn't sure what kind of trouble.

He focused again on Cam. "What about the wait-staff?" Normally, Tiffany would be in the main bar taking care of the customers who sat at tables. "He didn't send them home, too, did he?"

"Oh, no," Cam said. "Tiffany and Aly are scheduled to be on until closing, and they're in the back with—"

But his last words were drowned out by a high-pitched squeal of "*You're here!*" and Reece looked up to find Jenna Montgomery—the woman he craved—barreling across the room and flinging herself into his arms.

Meet Damien Stark

Only his passion could set her free…

Release Me
Claim Me
Complete Me
Anchor Me
Lost With Me

Meet Damien Stark in Release Me, *book 1 of the wildly sensual series that's left millions of readers breathless …*

Chapter One

A cool ocean breeze caresses my bare shoulders, and I shiver, wishing I'd taken my roommate's advice and brought a shawl with me tonight. I arrived in Los Angeles only four days ago, and I haven't yet adjusted to the concept of summer temperatures changing with the setting of the sun. In Dallas, June is hot, July is hotter, and August is hell.

Not so in California, at least not by the beach. LA Lesson Number One: Always carry a sweater if you'll be out after dark.

Of course, I could leave the balcony and go back inside to the party. Mingle with the millionaires. Chat up the celebrities. Gaze dutifully at the paintings. It is a gala art opening, after all, and my boss brought me here to meet and greet and charm and chat. Not to lust over the panorama that is coming alive in front of me. Bloodred clouds bursting against the pale orange sky. Blue-gray waves shimmering with dappled gold.

I press my hands against the balcony rail and lean forward, drawn to the intense, unreachable beauty of the setting sun. I regret that I didn't bring the battered Nikon I've had since high school. Not that it would have fit in my itty-bitty beaded purse. And a bulky camera bag paired with a little black dress is a big, fat fashion no-no.

But this is my very first Pacific Ocean sunset, and I'm determined to document the moment. I pull out my iPhone and snap a picture.

"Almost makes the paintings inside seem redundant, doesn't it?" I recognize the throaty, feminine voice and turn to face Evelyn Dodge, retired actress turned agent turned patron of the arts—and my hostess for the evening.

"I'm so sorry. I know I must look like a giddy tourist, but we don't have sunsets like this in Dallas."

"Don't apologize," she says. "I pay for that view every month when I write the mortgage check. It damn well better be spectacular."

I laugh, immediately more at ease.

"Hiding out?"

"Excuse me?"

"You're Carl's new assistant, right?" she asks, referring to my boss of three days.

"Nikki Fairchild."

"I remember now. Nikki from Texas." She looks me up and down, and I wonder if she's disappointed that I don't have big hair and cowboy boots. "So who does he want you to charm?"

"Charm?" I repeat, as if I don't know exactly what she means.

She cocks a single brow. "Honey, the man would rather walk on burning coals than come to an art show. He's fishing for investors and you're the bait." She makes a rough noise in the back of her throat. "Don't worry. I won't press you to tell me who. And I don't blame you for hiding out. Carl's brilliant, but he's a bit of a prick."

"It's the brilliant part I signed on for," I say, and she barks out a laugh.

The truth is that she's right about me being the bait. "Wear a cocktail dress," Carl had said. "Something flirty."

Seriously? I mean, *Seriously?*

I should have told him to wear his own damn cocktail dress. But I didn't. Because I want this job. I fought to get this job. Carl's company, C-Squared Technologies, successfully launched three web-based products in the last eighteen months. That track record had caught the industry's eye, and Carl had been hailed as a man to watch.

More important from my perspective, that meant he was a man to learn from, and I'd prepared for the job interview with an intensity bordering on obsession. Landing the position had been a huge coup for me. So what if he wanted me to wear something flirty? It was a small price to pay.

Shit.

"I need to get back to being the bait," I say.

"Oh, hell. Now I've gone and made you feel either guilty or self-conscious. Don't be. Let them get liquored up in there first. You catch more flies with alcohol anyway. Trust me. I know."

She's holding a pack of cigarettes, and now she taps one out, then extends the pack to me. I shake my head. I love the smell of tobacco—it reminds me of my grandfather—but actually inhaling the smoke does nothing for me.

"I'm too old and set in my ways to quit," she says. "But God forbid I smoke in my own damn house. I swear, the mob would burn me in effigy. You're not going to start lecturing me on the dangers of second-hand smoke, are you?"

"No," I promise.

"Then how about a light?"

I hold up the itty-bitty purse. "One lipstick, a credit card, my driver's license, and my phone."

"No condom?"

"I didn't think it was that kind of party," I say dryly.

"I knew I liked you." She glances around the balcony. "What the hell kind of party am I throwing if I don't even have one goddamn candle on one goddamn table? Well, fuck it." She puts the unlit cigarette to her mouth and inhales, her eyes closed and her expression rapturous. I can't help but like her. She wears hardly any makeup, in stark contrast to all the other women here tonight, myself included, and her dress is more of a caftan, the batik pattern as interesting as the woman herself.

She's what my mother would call a brassy broad —loud, large, opinionated, and self-confident. My mother would hate her. I think she's awesome.

She drops the unlit cigarette onto the tile and grinds it with the toe of her shoe. Then she signals to one of the catering staff, a girl dressed all in black and carrying a tray of champagne glasses.

The girl fumbles for a minute with the sliding door that opens onto the balcony, and I imagine those flutes tumbling off, breaking against the hard tile, the scattered shards glittering like a wash of diamonds.

I picture myself bending to snatch up a broken stem. I see the raw edge cutting into the soft flesh at the base of my thumb as I squeeze. I watch myself clutching it tighter, drawing strength from the pain, the way some people might try to extract luck from a rabbit's foot.

The fantasy blurs with memory, jarring me with its potency. It's fast and powerful, and a little disturbing because I haven't needed the pain in a long time, and I don't understand why I'm thinking about it now, when I feel steady and in control.

I am fine, I think. *I am fine, I am fine, I am fine.*

"Take one, honey," Evelyn says easily, holding a flute out to me.

I hesitate, searching her face for signs that my mask has slipped and she's caught a glimpse of my rawness. But her face is clear and genial.

"No, don't you argue," she adds, misinterpreting my hesitation. "I bought a dozen cases and I hate to see good alcohol go to waste. Hell no," she adds when the girl tries to hand her a flute. "I hate the stuff. Get me a vodka. Straight up. Chilled. Four olives. Hurry up, now. Do you want me to dry up like a leaf and float away?"

The girl shakes her head, looking a bit like a twitchy, frightened rabbit. Possibly one that had sacrificed his foot for someone else's good luck.

Evelyn's attention returns to me. "So how do you like LA? What have you seen? Where have you been? Have you bought a map of the stars yet? Dear God, tell me you're not getting sucked into all that tourist bullshit."

"Mostly I've seen miles of freeway and the inside of my apartment."

"Well, that's just sad. Makes me even more glad that Carl dragged your skinny ass all the way out here tonight."

I've put on fifteen welcome pounds since the years when my mother monitored every tiny thing that went in my mouth, and while I'm perfectly happy with my size-eight ass, I wouldn't describe it as skinny. I know Evelyn means it as a compliment, though, and so I smile. "I'm glad he brought me, too. The paintings really are amazing."

"Now don't do that—don't you go sliding into the polite-conversation routine. No, no," she says before I can protest. "I'm sure you mean it. Hell, the paintings are wonderful. But you're getting the flat-eyed look of a girl on her best behavior, and we can't have that. Not when I was getting to know the real you."

"Sorry," I say. "I swear I'm not fading away on you."

Because I genuinely like her, I don't tell her that she's wrong—she hasn't met the real Nikki Fairchild. She's met Social Nikki who, much like Malibu Barbie, comes with a complete set of accessories. In my case, it's not a bikini and a convertible. Instead, I have the *Elizabeth Fairchild Guide for Social Gatherings*.

My mother's big on rules. She claims it's her Southern upbringing. In my weaker moments, I agree. Mostly, I just think she's a controlling bitch. Since the first time she took me for tea at the Mansion at Turtle Creek in Dallas at age three, I have had the rules drilled into my head. How to walk, how to talk, how to dress. What to eat, how much to drink, what kinds of jokes to tell.

I have it all down, every trick, every nuance, and I wear my practiced pageant smile like armor against the world. The result being that I don't think I could truly be myself at a party even if my life depended on it.

This, however, is not something Evelyn needs to know.

"Where exactly are you living?" she asks.

"Studio City. I'm sharing a condo with my best friend from high school."

"Straight down the 101 for work and then back home again. No wonder you've only seen concrete. Didn't anyone tell you that you should have taken an apartment on the Westside?"

"Too pricey to go it alone," I admit, and I can tell that my admission surprises her. When I make the effort—like when I'm Social Nikki—I can't help but look like I come from money. Probably because I do.

Come from it, that is. But that doesn't mean I brought it with me.

"How old are you?"

"Twenty-four."

Evelyn nods sagely, as if my age reveals some secret about me. "You'll be wanting a place of your own soon enough. You call me when you do and we'll find you someplace with a view. Not as good as this one, of course, but we can manage something better than a freeway on-ramp."

"It's not that bad, I promise."

"Of course it's not," she says in a tone that says the exact opposite. "As for views," she continues, gesturing toward the now-dark ocean and the sky that's starting to bloom with stars, "you're welcome to come back anytime and share mine."

"I might take you up on that," I admit. "I'd love to bring a decent camera back here and take a shot or two."

"It's an open invitation. I'll provide the wine and you can provide the entertainment. A young woman loose in the city. Will it be a drama? A rom-com? Not a tragedy, I hope. I love a good cry as much as the next woman, but I like you. You need a happy ending."

I tense, but Evelyn doesn't know she's hit a nerve. That's why I moved to LA, after all. New life. New story. New Nikki.

I ramp up the Social Nikki smile and lift my

champagne flute. "To happy endings. And to this amazing party. I think I've kept you from it long enough."

"Bullshit," she says. "I'm the one monopolizing you, and we both know it."

We slip back inside, the buzz of alcohol-fueled conversation replacing the soft calm of the ocean.

"The truth is, I'm a terrible hostess. I do what I want, talk to whoever I want, and if my guests feel slighted they can damn well deal with it."

I gape. I can almost hear my mother's cries of horror all the way from Dallas.

"Besides," she continues, "this party isn't supposed to be about me. I put together this little shindig to introduce Blaine and his art to the community. He's the one who should be doing the mingling, not me. I may be fucking him, but I'm not going to baby him."

Evelyn has completely destroyed my image of how a hostess for the not-to-be-missed social event of the weekend is supposed to behave, and I think I'm a little in love with her for that.

"I haven't met Blaine yet. That's him, right?" I point to a tall reed of a man. He is bald, but sports a red goatee. I'm pretty sure it's not his natural color. A small crowd hums around him, like bees drawing nectar from a flower. His outfit is certainly as bright as one.

"That's my little center of attention, all right," Evelyn says. "The man of the hour. Talented, isn't he?" Her hand sweeps out to indicate her massive living room. Every wall is covered with paintings. Except for a few benches, whatever furniture was once in the room has been removed and replaced with easels on which more paintings stand.

I suppose technically they are portraits. The models are nudes, but these aren't like anything you would see in a classical art book. There's something edgy about them. Something provocative and raw. I can tell that they are expertly conceived and carried out, and yet they disturb me, as if they reveal more about the person viewing the portrait than about the painter or the model.

As far as I can tell, I'm the only one with that reaction. Certainly the crowd around Blaine is glowing. I can hear the gushing praise from here.

"I picked a winner with that one," Evelyn says. "But let's see. Who do you want to meet? Rip Carrington and Lyle Tarpin? Those two are guaranteed drama, that's for damn sure, and your roommate will be jealous as hell if you chat them up."

"She will?"

Evelyn's brows arch up. "Rip and Lyle? They've been feuding for weeks." She narrows her eyes at me. "The fiasco about the new season of their sitcom? It's all over the Internet? You really don't know them?"

"Sorry," I say, feeling the need to apologize. "My school schedule was pretty intense. And I'm sure you can imagine what working for Carl is like."

Speaking of …

I glance around, but I don't see my boss anywhere.

"That is one serious gap in your education," Evelyn says. "Culture—and yes, pop culture counts— is just as important as—what did you say you studied?"

"I don't think I mentioned it. But I have a double major in electrical engineering and computer science."

"So you've got brains and beauty. See? That's something else we have in common. Gotta say, though, with an education like that, I don't see why you signed up to be Carl's secretary."

I laugh. "I'm not, I swear. Carl was looking for someone with tech experience to work with him on the business side of things, and I was looking for a job where I could learn the business side. Get my feet wet. I think he was a little hesitant to hire me at first—my skills definitely lean toward tech—but I convinced him I'm a fast learner."

She peers at me. "I smell ambition."

I lift a shoulder in a casual shrug. "It's Los Angeles. Isn't that what this town is all about?"

"Ha! Carl's lucky he's got you. It'll be interesting to see how long he keeps you. But let's see … who here would intrigue you …?"

She casts about the room, finally pointing to a fifty-something man holding court in a corner. "That's

Charles Maynard," she says. "I've known Charlie for years. Intimidating as hell until you get to know him. But it's worth it. His clients are either celebrities with name recognition or power brokers with more money than God. Either way, he's got all the best stories."

"He's a lawyer?"

"With Bender, Twain & McGuire. Very prestigious firm."

"I know," I say, happy to show that I'm not entirely ignorant, despite not knowing Rip or Lyle. "One of my closest friends works for the firm. He started here but he's in their New York office now."

"Well, come on, then, Texas. I'll introduce you." We take one step in that direction, but then Evelyn stops me. Maynard has pulled out his phone, and is shouting instructions at someone. I catch a few well-placed curses and eye Evelyn sideways. She looks unconcerned "He's a pussycat at heart. Trust me, I've worked with him before. Back in my agenting days, we put together more celebrity biopic deals for our clients than I can count. And we fought to keep a few tell-alls off the screen, too." She shakes her head, as if reliving those glory days, then pats my arm. "Still, we'll wait 'til he calms down a bit. In the meantime, though …"

She trails off, and the corners of her mouth turn down in a frown as she scans the room again. "I don't think he's here yet, but—oh! Yes! Now *there's* someone you should meet. And if you want to talk views, the house he's building has one that makes my view look like, well, like yours." She points toward the entrance hall, but all I see are bobbing heads and haute couture. "He hardly ever accepts invitations, but we go way back," she says.

I still can't see who she's talking about, but then the crowd parts and I see the man in profile. Goose bumps rise on my arms, but I'm not cold. In fact, I'm suddenly very, very warm.

He's tall and so handsome that the word is almost an insult. But it's more than that. It's not his looks, it's his *presence*. He commands the room simply by being in it, and I realize that Evelyn and I aren't the only ones looking at him. The entire crowd has noticed his arrival. He must feel the weight of all those eyes, and yet the attention doesn't faze him at all. He smiles at the girl with the champagne, takes a glass, and begins to chat casually with a woman who approaches him, a simpering smile stretched across her face.

"Damn that girl," Evelyn says. "She never did bring me my vodka."

But I barely hear her. "Damien Stark," I say. My voice surprises me. It's little more than breath.

Evelyn's brows rise so high I notice the movement in my peripheral vision. "Well, how about that?" she says knowingly. "Looks like I guessed right."

"You did," I admit. "Mr. Stark is just the man I want to see."

I hope you enjoyed the excerpt! Grab your own copy of Release Me … or any of the books in the series now!

The Original Trilogy
Release Me
Claim Me
Complete Me
And Beyond...
Anchor Me
Lost With Me

More Nikki & Damien Stark

Need your Nikki & Damien fix?

Not only is *Please Me*, a 1001 Dark Nights Nikki & Damien Stark novella releasing August 28, 2018, but there's a brand new *full length* Nikki & Damien book coming in 2018, too!

Lost With Me
Stark Saga, Book 5
Coming Fall 2018

I just get sucked into these books and can not get enough of this series. They are so well written and as satisfying as each book is they leave you greedy for more. — Goodreads reviewer on *Wicked Torture*

A sizzling, intoxicating, sexy read!!!! J. Kenner had me devouring Wicked Dirty, the second installment of *Stark World Series* in one sitting. I loved everything about this book from the opening pages to the raw and vulnerable characters. With her sophisticated prose, Kenner created a love story that had the perfect blend of lust, passion, sexual tension, raw emotions and love. - Michelle, Four Chicks Flipping Pages

Wicked Dirty CLAIMED and CONSUMED every ounce of me from the very first page. Mind racing. Pulse pounding. Breaths bated. Feels flowing. Eyes wide in anticipation. Heart beating out of my chest. I felt the current of *Wicked Dirty* flow through me. I was DRUNK on this book that was my fine whiskey, so smooth and spectacular, and could not get enough of this *Wicked Dirty* drink. - Karen Bookalicious Babes Blog

"Sinfully sexy and full of heart. Kenner shines in this second chance, slow burn of a romance. Wicked

Grind is the perfect book to kick off your summer."-
K. Bromberg, New York Times bestselling author (on Wicked Grind)

"J. Kenner never disappoints~her books just get better and better." - *Mom's Guilty Pleasure (on Wicked Grind)*

"I don't think J. Kenner could write a bad story if she tried. ... Wicked Grind is a great beginning to what I'm positive will be a very successful series. ... The line forms here." *iScream Books (On Wicked Grind)*

"Scorching, sweet, and soul-searing, *Anchor Me* is the ultimate love story that stands the test of time and tribulation. THE TRUEST LOVE!" *Bookalicious Babes Blog (on Anchor Me)*

"J. Kenner has brought this couple to life and the character connection that I have to these two holds no bounds and that is testament to J. Kenner's writing ability." *The Romance Cover (on Anchor Me)*

"J. Kenner writes an emotional and personal story line. ... The premise will captivate your imagination; the characters will break your heart; the romance continues to push the envelope." *The Reading Café (on Anchor Me)*

"Kenner may very well have cornered the market on sinfully attractive, dominant antiheroes and the women who swoon for them . . ." *Romantic Times*

"*Wanted* is another J. Kenner masterpiece . . . This was an intriguing look at self-discovery and forbidden love all wrapped into a neat little action-suspense package. There was plenty of sexual tension and eventually action. Evan was hot, hot, hot! Together, they were combustible. But can we expect anything less from J. Kenner?" *Reading Haven*

"*Wanted* by J. Kenner is the whole package! A toe-curling smokin' hot read, full of incredible characters and a brilliant storyline that you won't be able to get enough of. I can't wait for the next book in this series . . . I'm hooked!" *Flirty & Dirty Book Blog*

"J. Kenner's evocative writing thrillingly captures the power of physical attraction, the pull of longing, the universe-altering effect one person can have on another. . . . *Claim Me* has the emotional depth to back up the sex . . . Every scene is infused with both erotic tension, and the tension of wondering what lies beneath Damien's veneer – and how and when it will be revealed." *Heroes and Heartbreakers*

"*Claim Me* by J. Kenner is an erotic, sexy and exciting ride. The story between Damien and Nikki is amazing and written beautifully. The intimate and detailed sex scenes will leave you fanning yourself to cool down. With the writing style of Ms. Kenner you almost feel like you are there in the story riding along the emotional rollercoaster with Damien and Nikki." *Fresh Fiction*

"PERFECT for fans of *Fifty Shades of Grey* and *Bared to You. Release Me* is a powerful and erotic romance novel that is sure to make adult romance readers sweat, sigh and swoon." *Reading, Eating & Dreaming Blog*

"I will admit, I am in the 'I loved *Fifty Shades*' camp, but after reading *Release Me*, Mr. Grey only scratches the surface compared to Damien Stark." *Cocktails and Books Blog*

"It is not often when a book is so amazingly well-written that I find it hard to even begin to accurately describe it . . . I recommend this book to everyone who is interested in a passionate love story." *Romance-bookworm's Reviews*

"The story is one that will rank up with the *Fifty Shades* and Cross Fire trilogies." *Incubus Publishing Blog*

"The plot is complex, the characters engaging, and J. Kenner's passionate writing brings it all perfectly together." *Harlequin Junkie*

Also by J. Kenner

The Stark Saga Novels:

Only his passion could set her free…

Meet Damien Stark

The Original Trilogy

Release Me

Claim Me

Complete Me

And Beyond…

Anchor Me

Lost With Me

Stark Ever After

(Stark Saga novellas):

Happily ever after is just the beginning.

The passion between Damien & Nikki continues.

Take Me

Have Me

Play My Game

Seduce Me

Unwrap Me

Shake It Up

All Night Long

In Too Deep

Light My Fire

Walk The Line

Bar Bites: A Man of the Month Cookbook(by J. Kenner & Suzanne M. Johnson)

Additional Titles

Wild Thing

One Night (A Stark World short story in the Second Chances anthology)

Also by Julie Kenner

The Protector (Superhero) Series:

The Cat's Fancy (prequel)

Aphrodite's Kiss

Aphrodite's Passion

Aphrodite's Secret

Aphrodite's Flame

Aphrodite's Embrace (novella)

Aphrodite's Delight (novella – free download)

Demon Hunting Soccer Mom Series:

Carpe Demon

California Demon

Demons Are Forever

Deja Demon

The Demon You Know (short story)

Demon Ex Machina

Pax Demonica

About the Author

J. Kenner (aka Julie Kenner) is the *New York Times*, *USA Today*, *Publishers Weekly*, *Wall Street Journal* and #1 International bestselling author of over eighty novels, novellas and short stories in a variety of genres.

JK has been praised by *Publishers Weekly* as an author with a "flair for dialogue and eccentric characterizations" and by *RT Bookclub* for having "cornered the market on sinfully attractive, dominant antiheroes and the women who swoon for them." A five-time finalist for Romance Writers of America's prestigious RITA award, JK took home the first RITA trophy awarded in the category of erotic romance in 2014 for her novel, *Claim Me* (book 2 of her Stark Trilogy).

In her previous career as an attorney, JK worked as a lawyer in Southern California and Texas. She currently lives in Central Texas, with her husband, two daughters, and two rather spastic cats.

More ways to connect:

www.jkenner.com
Text JKenner to 21000 for JK's text alerts.

 facebook.com/jkennerbooks

twitter.com/juliekenner

CPSIA information can be obtained
at www.ICGtesting.com
Printed in the USA
LVOW10s2008080518
576442LV00011B/1334/P